DATE DUE			
FEB 12 1984			
OCT 08 1999			
MY 03 '04			
MY 12 '04			
5-18-04			

Brother Night

Victor Kelleher

Illustrated by Peter Clarke

Walker and Company
New York

First published in the United States of America in 1991
by Walker Publishing Company, Inc.

Published simultaneously in Canada by Thomas Allen & Son
Canada, Limited, Markham, Ontario

Library of Congress Cataloging-in-Publication Data

Kelleher, Victor, 1939–
Brother Night / Victor Kelleher.
p.   cm.
Summary: Rabon and his monstrous brother Lal journey to the twin
cities to discover their destiny at the hands of the Sun Lord and
the Night Lord.
ISBN 0-8027-8100-4
[1. Fantasy.]   I. Title.
PZ7.K28127Br   1991
[Fic]—dc20   90-19743
CIP
AC

Printed in the United States of America

2   4   6   8   10   9   7   5   3   1

This work was assisted by a writers' fellowship from the Australian Council, the Federal
Government's arts funding and advisory body.

Contents

Chapter One
Arrivals

"It all began with the knocking at the gate," Dorf explained to his son. "I remember it well. An evening some months before you were born. It was the end of a particularly hot day, and I'd no sooner swung the gate closed and locked the wheel into position than the knocking started up, loud enough to wake the dead."

Rabon, who never tired of hearing the old man's story, edged forward on his seat, his eyes bright with anticipation. "What happened next?" he asked eagerly.

"Why, I called for whoever it was to wait until morning," Dorf replied. "But I could have saved my breath for all the good it did. The knocking just went on, louder than before. So in the end I climbed the ladder to see who was out there. Not that it helped much. You know what it's like up there on the tower in the early evening: the setting sun can be dazzling. All I could see was the bent figure of a woman in a tattered robe. I thought at first she was one of the mountain folk, here to beg from us. And I certainly wasn't opening the gate for the likes of them. I told her as much; how she'd have to wait until sunrise if she—"

"And what did she say?" Rabon cut in, his face flushed in the candlelight.

Dorf, as always, refused to be rushed by the impatience of his teenage son. "You know as well as I do what happened," he replied. "You've heard it all often enough."

"Tell me again," the boy demanded, an edge of anger, never far beneath the surface, breaking through his voice.

Dorf studied his son in the dim light, his own face revealing a mixture of affection and disapproval. "If you want to hear the story so badly," he said, "why not ask Jenna for her version?"

As he knew it would, Jenna's name had a dampening effect on the boy, and in his own time he continued with his story.

"Now where was I?" he murmured vaguely. "Ah yes, I'd just sent her packing. Or rather I'd tried to. But she was no ordinary visitor. I guessed that when she stepped back, right in amongst the nest of snakes that always lies curled up in the dust beside the wall. Anyone else would have leaped clear, but not her. She just stood there. And the creatures themselves were as docile as you please, slithering peacefully around her feet."

Dorf plucked at his lower lip, his aging face lost in thought as he recalled that fateful encounter, which, for him especially, had proved so important.

"No, there was nothing ordinary about her," he repeated. "She made that obvious straight away. She didn't bother to plead or beg, as you'd expect. Instead, she invoked the Night Lord. Ordered me, in his name, to open the gate. In his name! She didn't whisper it either. She came right out with it, showing no more concern for him than she had for the snakes — even then, with the dusk closing around us."

Rabon, hanging on every word, shivered slightly and cast a nervous glance at the shadows gathered in the corners of the room.

"Well, I couldn't decide what to do," Dorf sighed. "Not for a moment or two anyway. It was different when she looked up and I saw her face. A clear view I had of it, in the last rays of the setting sun."

He was immediately aware of the boy's eyes turned questioningly toward him.

"You wonder why her face should have made a difference?" he added quickly. "That's because you're used to her. But bear in mind, no one in the village had ever seen a priestess of the twin cities. That tattoo of hers gave me a shock, I can tell you, the way it ran right across her forehead and down the bridge of her nose. Also, she was a lot younger in those days, her skin unlined, so the design stood out more boldly—the rod showing thick and blue, with the two snakes coiled tightly around it."

He shook his head at the memory.

"One glimpse was enough," he confessed. "Turning her away would have been like spurning the Sun Lord himself. Faster than you can say his name, I was down the ladder and spinning the wheel to let her in. I was glad I had, because I soon discovered she was scared as well as tired. As she limped through the gate, she looked behind her, out across the dry plain, and there was real fear in her eyes."

"Fear?" Rabon inched closer to the old man. "What was out there?"

"Nothing that I could see. And it wasn't just the coming dusk that troubled her, for I'll tell you something else. When I offered her the gift of fresh water, gathered that same morning from the pool beside the swamp, she called on the Night Lord yet again. Spoke his name right here in this room. 'May he look kindly upon you,' she said. I ask you, what kind of thanks was that?"

For once, Rabon showed no readiness to respond; while Dorf, still caught up in the events of that momentous night, stared moodily into the candle flame. What he saw within its flickering light was himself, all those years ago, standing watch over the sleeping figure of his unexpected guest; her tattooed face, divided by a shaft of moonlight, filling him with wonder. Once more the mystery of her presence seemed to invade the room. Why had she, a priestess of the twin cities, journeyed alone to his village? What had drawn her from the service of the Sun Lord, up through the withering winds that scoured the mountain passes, and across the dead plain?

Those same questions, which had so puzzled him then, remained with him still, though now he admitted none of his lingering anxiety to his son. With a toss of the head, he tore his eyes from the flame and finished the first part of his story by saying simply:

"Anyway, there you have it. That was how Jenna came to our village."

Rabon, only partly satisfied, pressed his bare shoulders back against the earth wall. "But all you've told me is the beginning," he complained. "What about the rest?"

Dorf scrubbed at his stubbly chin. "You know that too. We built her a house, and in return she became a midwife to the women."

"Yes, but what else?"

"You mean the part about the swamp?"

Rabon nodded excitedly. "Tell me that part again."

The old man shrugged. "She ignored the time-honored warnings and started going there regularly. Not just to the pool, but deep into the swamp itself. To where the mist rises and the gnarled trees grow thick around the stagnant hollows. Where only—"

"Did she see him?" Rabon broke in, the excitement in his voice mingled now with dread. "Was he in there waiting for her?"

"Who knows?" Dorf replied, shrinking from a direct answer. "She claimed she went there only to collect roots and herbs for her medicines. That's still the reason she gives. It may be true. No one denies she's a great healer. But . . ."

"Yes?" Rabon prompted him.

Dorf guessed what the boy was waiting to hear, and with a sigh, partly of sadness, partly of resignation, he went on: "Son, after she started visiting the swamp, she showed signs of being with child." He sighed again. "At first people said it was fathered by one of the priests in the city, though that didn't explain why she'd run off and hidden herself in an out-of-the-way place like this village. No, it couldn't have been as simple as that. So then some of the gossips began whispering about the Sun Lord—how *he* must be the father."

"Was he?" Rabon asked wistfully.

"They may have been right," he murmured. "For I've never seen a fairer child than Jenna's first-born. As radiant as the sun it was." He turned his head away, yet still, from the corner of one eye, he glimpsed Rabon's watchful face, the boy's hair flashing gold in the candlelight. "Minutes after its birth," he continued hastily, "the old women carried it outside for everyone to see. At the sight of it, people began to laugh with joy. Or was it relief? Some of them even broke into song, the whole village rejoicing until . . . until . . ."

He paused and leaned toward the candle, which was burning badly, sending threatening shadows darting across the walls and low ceiling. With his finger and thumb he nipped off the ragged end of the wick, allowing the flame to settle. As he leaned back, he was conscious not only of Rabon's fierce eyes fixed upon his, but of the stillness of the night hovering like a phantom just beyond the window space. From the distant swamp there sounded a single owl hoot, so doleful it might almost have been a warning.

"Yes," he muttered, "we were happy for a while. Until we heard Jenna moaning and crying. That changed things quick enough. 'Why can't she rejoice like the rest of us?' we complained. Me as loud as any. After all, she'd just given birth to a child of the Sun Lord. It seemed to us she should have been more pleased than anyone." He took a shuddering breath, to steady himself. "That's when the old women told us. The truth. About the twin. The other one, yet to be born."

"His!" Rabon hissed. "Him! Watching in the swamp!"

"A monstrous thing it was!" Dorf groaned. "Such a head on it, Jenna shrieked aloud when it burst into the world. As dark as the other one was fair. So foul and ugly you'd hardly think it was human, and with a body already twice the size of its twin, like some . . . some terrible giant in the making. No, an ogre! A great twisted shape that had somehow escaped from our dreams."

"His!" Rabon repeated. "Luan's!"

The old man's head shot up, his deep-set eyes glancing first at his son and then warily out into the night. "Only a fool speaks that name," he whispered in disapproval. "Some say the mention of it is enough to conjure him. Especially when the moon's near the full. And remember, he has little reason for looking kindly on the people here. Not after what we did to his son."

"Tell me that part too," Rabon insisted, though all the eagerness had gone from his manner now. His lips were pulled tight across his teeth and he had edged further into the room, as though shrinking from the dark space of the open window.

"It was the worst day of my life," Dorf confessed. "And the best," he added, but so softly that the words failed to carry to his son. "Many of the people were all for killing both children there and then. They might have done but for Jenna. You should have seen her, the way she held both babies fiercely against her. The golden child and that black, squirming thing of the night. Protecting them both equally, as though each was a gift from heaven. Clawing at the women when they came near."

"So it was her doing that one of them was saved?" Rabon asked hopefully.

Dorf made as if to shake his head, but stopped as he saw a trace of disappointment flit across the boy's face. "I suppose you could say that," he agreed hesitantly. "If she hadn't fought so hard, the people may not have taken pity on her. And it was pity that saved the first-born. 'Let it live,' they said, 'but not with the witch.'"

"And the second child?" Rabon asked in a breathless whisper. "The Night Lord's monster son?"

Dorf tried but failed to suppress the shudder that trembled through him. With one hand shielding his eyes, his chin sunk onto his chest, he muttered unhappily, "It was taken deep into the swamp. To a place of darkness. Where the sun itself shines with only the pallor of the moon."

"To be killed?" The longing in Rabon's voice was unmistakable.

Not for the first time that evening, Dorf frowned with disapproval. "The one appointed to carry the child was ordered to kill it," he conceded. Then, his voice softening: "But who can say whether he obeyed the order? As monstrous as the child was, it was alive. Moving in his hands. Its great mouth reaching for the nipple it would never suck." A half-stifled sob broke from him, and he ducked his head even lower, as though avoiding the feeble glimmer of the candle flame.

"So he spared it," Rabon stated flatly.

"I'm not saying that," Dorf answered in a firmer tone. "All I'm saying is that he may have left it there. Placed it beside some pool, amongst the twisted roots of a great tree."

"Spared it," the boy repeated, as flatly as before.

Dorf swung forward, his hand raised, but as always, confronted by the boy's golden hair, his handsome olive-skinned face, he could not bring himself to strike.

"Do you call it an act of mercy to leave the child there alone?" he cried hoarsely. "If hunger and exposure didn't kill it, there were other things to complete the task. Huge water snakes hanging from the trees, black scorpions lurking in the scum on the surface of the pools, deadly spiders hidden amongst the roots and fallen leaves. And if they weren't danger enough, still there was the fever that rises with the mist each evening." He shook his head. "No, there was no mercy in such a deed. It was worthy of punishment, not of the blessing that followed."

"Blessing?" The word spoken with a sharpness that reminded him of Jenna.

"Yes, a blessing," he said decisively, and reached out to brush his fingers gently against the boy's cheek. "You see . . . you see . . . the person who carried the monster child to the swamp . . . he also took Jenna's first-born into his care. To raise him as . . . as his own son."

It was the only time he had ever made that admission. Now, with a growing sense of loss, he waited for the inevitable question.

Yet it never came. The boy sucked in his breath once, sharply, and that was all. Moments later, without any further comment, he crossed the room and lay down on the narrower of the two beds against the far wall.

With a sigh, Dorf stood up and snuffed out the candle—the darkness, the pungent odor of the spent wick enclosing him instantly. "Tonight, I want to tell you something else," he murmured, speaking to the shadowy room. "Something important. As far as I'm concerned, you will always be my son. Always. No matter what anyone says."

Still there was no reply, and eventually he too crossed the room and lay down, the bed creaking as he settled comfortably; his regular breathing soon indicated that he was asleep.

Only then did Rabon move. Rising noiselessly, he padded out of the house and up the ladder to the top of the tower.

The night was particularly dark, the moon covered by a bank of cloud. To the west he could see nothing: the dry plain and far-off mountains shrouded in a blackness that made him shudder. With a quick, nervous motion he turned toward the east, to where the closely set mud dwellings of the village lay clustered beneath him. At such an hour he had no difficulty in picking out one particular dwelling from all the rest. Jenna's.

On this night, as on any other, a light continued to show at her window, shining on long after the rest of the village was sunk in sleep. "Moon Witch" was what he had called her throughout his childhood, he and the other children chanting the name aloud whenever they saw her, and her house they had always referred to as, "the witch's parlor." Gazing at it now, he pictured to himself the woman inside—her tattooed face hollowed out by sickness. "Mother . . ." he murmured uncertainly, as though testing the word upon himself. Then, with even less certainty, his young face wrinkling up with disgust: "Brother . . ."

The word had barely passed his lips when the moon broke suddenly free of the cloud and shed its pale light upon the plain. There was no opportunity for Rabon to run and hide, or even to pretend he had not seen what lay beyond the eastern wall: the ominous black shadow of the swamp, its ragged treetops tipped magically with silver.

"Brother . . ." he repeated in a horrified whisper. And with a whimpering cry, of confusion and pain, he hunkered down on the platform, his face buried in his hands.

Chapter Two
A Gift

He had vowed to ignore her, or at least to treat her as he would any other woman in the village. Yet the next morning, before sunrise, when he heard her faltering footsteps approaching the gate, he could not resist going to the open doorway and looking out. She was no longer the vigorous healthy woman he remembered from his early childhood. Worn down by fever, her body was gaunt, her face skeleton-thin, her movements slow and painful. Watching her hobble through the gray dawn light, he was tempted to run out and help her. What dissuaded him—prompting him to duck back out of sight— was the way she suddenly stopped and swung around, as though half aware she was being spied on.

Peering now through a crack between the door-frame and the wall, he could see that despite her sickness her face was as fierce as ever, her gray eyes just as steady and piercing. Though while she remained gazing toward his house, her features softened slightly becoming al- most tender. Even the vivid tattoo, of a viper and a water snake entwined, seemed to lose some of its hard outline. Then she had turned away and resumed her slow progress, using her staff to flick aside an adder that lay coiled in the dust, its ropelike body still cold and sluggish at that time of morning.

She was no sooner through the gate than Rabon ran to the ladder
and scrambled up to the lookout post. Dorf, as usual, was already
there, standing guard, much as his father and grandfather had done
before him. At the sound of Rabon's approach he turned cheerfully;
but seeing the expression on the boy's face—the way his eyes were
fixed keenly, almost hungrily, on Jenna's retreating figure—he said
nothing, allowing his son to break the silence between them.

"Is there no cure for the fever?" Rabon asked at last.

Jenna had by then disappeared in the direction of the swamp, her
limping form hidden by the southern wall of the village. Only her
shadow was still visible, a dark line cast far across the plain by the
newly risen sun.

"A cure?" Dorf shook his head regretfully. "None that I've heard
of."

He kept his face averted as he spoke, knowing from long experience
the effect his words would have: how the youthful cheeks would flame
red, the blue eyes cloud over with passion.

"So why does she keep going there?" Rabon burst out. "Doesn't
she realize what that place is doing to her?"

"I expect she realizes it well enough," Dorf answered softly. "But
like all of us she has her work to do. Ours is to guard the gate. Hers,
as she understands it, is to gather healing plants from the swamp. She
may not be able to save herself, but she can go on saving others.
That's what draws her back there."

"Or is it him?" Rabon asked bitterly. "The Night Lord? Is he her
real reason for going back?"

"Hush, boy!" Dorf cautioned him. "Such thoughts are unworthy of
you. In any case, the Night Lord dwells far from here. He's a prisoner
in the Forbidden City. Every child knows that."

"His spirit then," Rabon insisted. "The hidden presence that fathered the monster. Does that still lure her to the swamp?"

Dorf grasped him roughly by the shoulders. "That's enough of such
talk!" he said in his sternest tone. "Whatever lurks in the swamp has
no use for her any longer. The two of them parted company before
you were born."

"That isn't what people are saying," Rabon countered. "I've heard them, the things they whisper. How she visits the swamp to laugh and talk with the Night Lord's spirit. Her 'familiar' — that's what they call it. There are some who claim they've seen —"

He never finished; Dorf's broad hand clamped over his mouth.

"I'm telling you they're liars!" he hissed. "And what's worse, they're lacking in kindness. After all she's done for this village, they should think better of her than that. Now especially, when she's sick and close to death."

He regretted his final words even as he uttered them. There was an uncomfortable pause, during which the sun climbed higher, flooding the bare plain with its hard yellow light. Already people were leaving the village to work in the irrigated fields bordering the swamp, and many of them called up to the old gatekeeper as they passed beneath.

"How close to death is she?" Rabon asked in a whisper.

Dorf pointed first to the sun and then to the gray shell of the moon hanging above the western horizon. "All things must pass," he said. "You, me, Jenna . . . everything."

"How long?"

Dorf pulled awkwardly at his lower lip. "I'm no healer, but I'd say . . . a week or two. No longer."

He finished speaking and braced himself for the expected outburst. But as on the previous evening, when he had admitted the truth about Rabon's birth, the boy's only sign of emotion was a sharp intake of breath.

For the rest of that morning Rabon brooded alone in the house. More than once Dorf called for him to take his share of the watch, but he ignored all the old man's entreaties. The one thing that seemed to rouse him was the return of the villagers from the fields.

That occurred soon after noon, when the growing heat of the day forced everyone to seek shelter. One after the other, in a long straggly line, they trooped wearily through the gate. Last of all came Jenna, her once firm stride reduced to a slow shuffle.

This time Rabon was not watching for her, but he was warned of her return by the chant of children's voices. "Moon Witch, Moon Witch!" they were shouting — a monotonous, jeering cry, accompanied by the rhythmic stamping of feet. Often, when he was younger, Rabon had joined in that same chant himself, but now the familiar sound brought him instantly to his feet, his cheeks flaming with anger.

Afterward, he was not able to say why he acted as he did. There was no moment of decision; no conscious choice to go to her. It was as if his body decided for him, sending him out through the door and into the blazing heat at a dead run.

"No, Rabon!" he heard someone cry, but whether it was Dorf's voice or Jenna's was unclear.

Within his line of vision children were dodging aside and scattering. All except one: a boy of his own age, the cooper's son whom he had played with in the shadow of the wall. The two of them — he and the boy — met with a jolting shock, each flailing at the other as they rolled over and over in the thick dust.

Dorf was the one who drew them apart. "Back to your house!" he cried angrily to the cooper's son. "And as for you . . . !"

He had turned his attention to Rabon, his arm already swinging down when Jenna's staff jerked forward, intercepting the blow.

"No, let the boy alone," she said sharply. "He didn't mean to act badly. It was his temper, that's all. The same passion as in all his kind."

Rabon had never seen Dorf humble himself before anyone. Yet he humbled himself then. Releasing his son, he muttered an apology and stumbled aside, bent low in a respectful bow.

"So . . ." she murmured, smiling at Rabon, "you have decided at last."

He did not know what to say, he and Jenna only a pace apart, caught there in a blazing circle of noonday heat. Slowly her face drew closer to his, her eyes questioning, as though waiting for him to speak. With undisguised tenderness she reached out to touch him — her fingertips already caressing his cheek when, from close by, there came a sneering laugh. And before Rabon could stop himself, he had struck her hand aside.

"Keep off, Moon Witch!" he heard himself cry, his own voice less familiar to him than the mocking laughter that continued in the background.

An instant later, his face red with shame, he had brushed past her and was running again: out of the gate and across the plain, ploughing doggedly through the loose sand until his breath failed and he could run no further. Wearily, he slumped to his knees, welcoming the searing touch of the hot sand on his bare legs, almost grateful for the way the scorching heat of the sun fell like a blow upon his shoulders.

That night, for the first time in years, Dorf beat him, laying six stinging stripes across the backs of his legs with his broad leather belt. He accepted the punishment without complaint, and Dorf, for his part, offered no explanation for what he was doing, his face sad-eyed and regretful as he swung the belt.

Some hours later Rabon's legs were still stinging painfully. Yet what kept him awake was a deeper kind of ache that he could not fully explain. Nearby, in the darkness, Dorf seemed equally troubled, for although asleep, he was groaning aloud. "Respect . . ." Rabon heard him mumble at one point, ". . . must have . . . for those . . . love . . ."

Those jumbled words were what decided him. For the second successive evening, he left the old man to his dreams and tiptoed to the door. The sight of the village, bathed in ghostly moonglow, made him hesitate, though only briefly. Moments later, his arms held shieldwise above his head to protect himself from the ever-present danger of the night, he hurried past the closed gate and across to the one dwelling that still showed a light.

She must have been expecting him because she answered his knock immediately. As the door swung open, a snake, lying dormant across the sill, reared up, but she coaxed it down with her bare hand and beckoned for him to enter.

The interior had none of the bareness of his own home. The walls were lined with shelves that held rows of jars and neat bundles of drying herbs and roots; the stamped earth floor was strewn with rushes gathered from the swamp. A door in the far wall led to a smaller room in which he could just make out two sun- or moon-shaped objects hanging from the ceiling. The faint breeze from the open doorway must have disturbed them because their polished metal faces winked briefly with reflected light.

"Well?" Jenna asked.

She was standing without the support of her staff, so bowed over by sickness that she had to look up at him. Even so, he found it impossible to meet her steady gaze.

"I've come to apologize," he said stiffly.

She broke into wheezy laughter. "Apologize for what? For calling me a Moon Witch? When that's what I am? What else . . . ?"

"No!" he cut in. "It isn't true. We're people of the sun. Both of us. How else could you . . . could I . . . ?" But he could not bring himself to go on.

She was watching him closely, the hint of a smile on her thin lips. "Why do you find it so hard to accept my allegiance to the Night Lord?" she asked curiously. Reaching to one side, she lifted the curtain covering the window. "Look out there," she instructed him. "Look at the moonlight. There's nothing fearful about it, never mind what the old stories say. See how cool and pale it is, how it casts a healing light onto the sun-withered plain. Like the swamp, which you also fear, it brings relief to a hot and thirsty land."

He had turned his head in order to look out, but his attention was caught by the sight of her hand so thin and frail, trembling even with the effort of holding aside the flimsy curtain.

"But enough of that," she added. "You didn't visit me for such talk. What really brought you here tonight?"

He succeeded at last in meeting her gaze. "I've come to . . . to find out who I am," he stammered nervously.

"That's easily answered. You're the gatekeeper's son. Who else?"

"No, who am I truly?"

She gave a low chuckle, which ended in a racking cough. "You forget there are many gates in this land of ours," she said at last. "Some great, some small. Each with a keeper of its own."

"There's only one keeper I want to hear about now," he said more confidently. "Solmak. The Sun Lord. Keeper of the greatest gate of all."

"Then you've come here on a fool's errand," she flashed back at him. "For he's the one creature on this earth I'll discuss with no one."

"Why not? What has he done to make you say that?"

He was watching her wasted face intently, but she merely shook her head, refusing to answer.

"So you can tell me nothing," he muttered, disappointed.

"Not true," she reprimanded him gently. "I can tell you that I'm your mother. That you're as dear to me as any son could be. Would you call that nothing?"

It was one of the things he had most wanted to hear from her lips. Yet still, although a surge of warm feeling swept through him, it was not enough. "And . . . and my twin?" he asked. "Was he also dear to you?"

Her face abruptly lost all its gentleness. "No mother should favor one son above the other," she said accusingly.

"But Dorf says he was a mon—"

"Hold your tongue!" she interrupted. "Or you might force me to choose between you. Also, like it or not, it's your brother you're speaking of."

He ducked his head as if she had struck him. He was already turning toward the door when she plucked at his sleeve.

"No, not yet," she pleaded, all the annoyance vanishing from her wasted features. "This may well be our last meeting. It's not a time for anger. We must say our farewells properly."

"Farewells?" He was unable to keep the grief from his voice. "Is that all you can leave me with? That and the memory of my dead brother? The Night Lord's child?"

She clicked her tongue in mild disapproval. "You speak like one who's been given nothing. What about the gift of life? Is that so little?"

"Something else," he begged—and in spite of himself he clutched at her hand and held it against his neck. "Some news of my father. You've lived in the halls of the Sun Lord. Been close to him. Only you can tell me what he's really like."

She hesitated for a second, and then she was tugging him by the shoulders, dragging him toward her, as though to protect him from some unseen evil. "Hasn't Dorf been father enough for you?" she cried unhappily.

His head was pressed so hard against her withered breasts he could hear the faltering beat of her heart. "I'm not denying Dorf!" he answered passionately. "I'd never do that. But I have a natural father too. And I know so little about him. A name—that's all he is to me."

His appeal must have affected her because her tight hold upon him slackened and she stepped away. She was swaying drunkenly now, exhausted by her exertion, her breath coming in uneven gasps.

"Very well," she panted. "Your father . . . don't ask me to name him . . . he . . . he . . ." With an effort, she gathered her remaining strength, driving the quaver from her voice. "This is the kind of man he is," she went on. "In all the years since your birth, he has never deserted you. Not in his heart. You've remained precious to him. And when the time comes, no matter how much you may hate or fear him, he'll be there. He won't fail you."

"Hate or fear him?" Rabon said, baffled. "I don't understand. Why should I . . . ?"

But her weakness and dizziness had returned and she was hardly listening. Groping for a nearby table, she leaned heavily upon it. "It's true," she whispered, "he won't fail you. And neither shall I."

It was as if she had reached some inner decision, for all at once she raised her head and looked directly at him. "We spoke earlier of gifts. And you were right in what you said then. This is a time for more than just farewells." With one trembling hand she felt inside her robe and drew something out. "Here," she said, "the second most important gift of all. A means of preserving the life you've been blessed with."

He stared down at what she was offering him: a charm carved from a piece of bone. It was quite large, covering most of her palm, with a small gold ring attached to one end and a strange hook or clasp at the other. The carving itself was of a snake: its head decorated with a jeweled eye; its long scaly body twisting and turning upon itself. The gaps between its many coils were cut completely away, allowing the candlelight to shine through.

"What is it?" he asked wonderingly.

"An ancient guide to those who are lost."

"A guide? To what?"

She waved a hand wearily. "To the Night Lord or the Sun Lord, whichever one you seek."

"And if I don't seek either of them?"

She laughed, not pleasantly, and might have fallen had he not steadied her. "Ah, but one of them will come looking for you," she whispered, her lips close to his ear. "You can be sure of that."

"Then why do I need this to guide me? And how does it work?"

"Questions! Nothing but questions!" she cried, shaking her head in distress. "When there's so little time . . . time . . ." She again reached into her robe and drew out a fine gold chain, which, with his help, she threaded through the ring at one end of the charm. "Come," she said more affectionately, slipping it over his head, "wear it close to your heart, in remembrance of me. And keep it secret. From him more than anyone else."

"Him? Do you mean Luan?"

But her strength had failed completely and she slumped into his arms. "When the time comes to use the charm," she whispered, "remember this, and remember it well: that the way lies only where the sun cannot reach. Let me hear you say it."

"The way lies only where the sun cannot reach," he repeated dutifully. "But what way do you . . . ?"

"Yes, that's it," she sighed in relief. "For both of you . . . both . . . when the two halves meet you must follow . . . follow only where the sun cannot . . . cannot . . ."

Her eyes had fallen closed, her head was lolling against his shoulder. Gently, for fear of hurting her, he tightened his arms around her waist and half carried her to the bed in the corner. She stirred once, briefly, as he eased her down—her eyes flickering open and gazing fondly at him.

"When he comes looking for you," she murmured, "remember this too . . . Fear those you would love, and love those you fear . . . Do you hear me? . . . love those you fear . . . when he comes . . ." Her voice faded slowly away and she was asleep.

Now, with no one to observe him, he bent down and kissed her tenderly on the forehead and both temples. Still she did not wake, her breath labored and uncertain in the silence, and sadly he crept to the door.

Just before he could leave, a movement in the far room caught his eye. The two round metal objects he had noticed earlier were circling around each other, set in motion by the sudden draft. As he watched, they clashed lightly together, giving out a high warning note. He glanced quickly at Jenna, but she slept on. Her face, half exposed to the candlelight, half in shadow, was like a mask evenly divided by the twin kingdoms of night and day.

That, although he did not realize it then, was the last time he was ever to see her alive.

Chapter Three
Voice from the Swamp

Rabon was on the tower with Dorf when the villagers came hurrying from the fields. It was an overcast day, much cooler than usual, and still only midafternoon—far too early for work to cease.

"Have my friends grown tired all of a sudden?" Dorf called teasingly. "Or are they so rich that they can afford to . . . ?"

He stopped as they drew closer and he saw the look of shock and terror in their eyes.

"Close the gate!" they called back, running through the broad opening in their eagerness to find safety.

Rabon had already scrambled down the ladder to meet them. "What is it?" he asked, alarmed.

One of the women, panting from her hurried journey, pointed back over the way she had come. "The spirit of the Night Lord," she explained. "He started howling near the edge of the swamp. We all heard it. A terrible noise."

"Some of us saw him," a man cut in. "Not more than a stone's throw from the pool."

Dorf, who had also descended the ladder, gave one last heaving turn to the great wheel that controlled the gate. "How can anyone *see* a spirit?" he asked doubtfully. "It's not a thing of flesh and blood like us."

"His shadow then," someone else explained. "That's what we saw. Passing swiftly between the trees."

But still Dorf was less than convinced. "A shadow?" he queried. "When the sun doesn't shine?"

"You can believe what you please," the first woman replied hotly. "We know what we saw. What we heard. The awful voice of the Night Lord, speaking through his spirit."

Like many of the others, she was already backing away, making for her own house — the door and window spaces throughout the village being rapidly closed up.

"Just make sure the gate stays shut," one last voice called out.

After that there was silence: the village empty and still except for a few snakes that stirred near the wall, and the occasional gusts of wind that disturbed the trodden dust. Even Rabon had begun to edge nervously toward the open doorway of their house.

Dorf turned on him sharply. "Where are *you* going? We're here to protect the community, not hide away. That's what it means to be a gatekeeper."

Shamed by Dorf's reprimand, Rabon stopped. "But you don't believe what the people said," he replied defensively. "I heard you. How it couldn't have been the Night Lord's spirit moving in the swamp. So what's the point of doubling the guard?"

Dorf, having secured the great wheel, was remounting the ladder. "Whatever I choose to believe," he called, continuing his upward climb, "still my duty remains the same. And so does yours. To guard the village from any threat of danger. With my life, if necessary."

So it was that they both stood vigil on the tower for the rest of the afternoon. Throughout that period their attention never flagged, their eyes fixed keenly on the swamp, which showed as a brilliant green stain upon the barren landscape. Only with the coming of dusk did they yawn and stretch and turn aside.

"As I suspected," Dorf muttered. "It was just their fear at work. Probably all they heard was an owl shrieking. Or the sigh of marsh gases rising up through the sodden earth."

Taking his words as a signal, Rabon turned with relief toward the ladder. Dorf, however, did not attempt to follow.

"You know my motto," he said, grinning apologetically. "Better safe than sorry. I'll stay on for a while longer, to make sure. You go ahead. Get some supper ready for us."

He spoke so easily and naturally that Rabon went without protest. Which was why, less than an hour later, the cry of alarm caught him by surprise.

Leaving what he was doing, he ran outside in time to see Dorf slide recklessly down the ladder, his feet hitting the ground with such force that he crumpled into the dust.

"We're invaded!" he shouted, scrambling up and making for the hoop of iron that hung beside the gate.

"Invaded? But the wall . . . no one could climb it without . . ."

"What I saw had no need to climb," the old man explained hoarsely. "It was just as they said—a shadow! Nothing more. It moved across the eastern wall like a dark cloud across the sky."

He had picked up an iron bar, which he brought crashing down upon the hoop, making a great clang that sounded through the village. Between gasping breaths, he swung the bar again and again, until the whole night was in uproar. Yet although a few doors opened a crack and a few lights blinked quickly on and off, no one emerged.

Gradually the noise subsided: the ringing falling to a low hum that sank at last to a faint vibration—something felt rather than heard. For a few seconds nothing disturbed the silence of the night; the unearthly hush muffled even the whirr of insect noise from the distant swamp. Then, from close at hand—so suddenly that Rabon and Dorf found themselves clinging to each other with fright—there arose a very different kind of noise: a long wailing note, like the sighing of a great wind, which rose and fell mournfully. High above them, the clouds thinned and parted, allowing a feeble wash of moonlight to filter through; by its ghostly light the wailing grew louder, more mournful, broken occasionally by a strange sobbing cry.

Dorf was the first to recover. "There!" he whispered, pointing to the blob of shadow that was Jenna's house. "There!"

Still gripping the iron bar, he ran to the other houses and beat at their doors. "Come out! Come out!" he shouted. "Prepare to defend the village!"

Slowly at first, the doors began to open: people emerged hesitantly; some armed with hoes and rakes others with axes and sticks or whatever lay at hand. In a fearful knot, crowded behind Dorf, they approached Jenna's door—the loud wailing, all the while, sounding eerily around them.

"Can you hear me, Jenna?" Dorf called. "We're here to help you. Let us in."

When there was no reply, he motioned for two men armed with axes to attack the door. It shuddered under the blows, the timber splitting and cracking, the planks crashing inward.

And still the wailing continued, so loud that the villagers held back. Only Rabon was drawn by the sound, by the terrible sadness in it. A sadness so deep and heartfelt that it seemed to wrench at him, to reach inside him and start into life an unspoken fear, to force a similar cry from his own lips.

Without being able to explain why, he began fighting his way through the crowd, pushing people aside in order to reach the doorway. The snake, which always guarded the sill, rose in his path and struck, but he had already leaped past, his feet sliding to a halt on the loosely strewn rushes; his eyes vainly probing the pitch-dark interior of the room.

He could hear the cry more clearly now: the quick intake of breath between the rising and falling notes; the faint swamp-odor of that same breath tainting the closed atmosphere. Then someone had thrust a brand of burning rushes through the doorway, filling the room with smoky light.

Rabon did not hear the cry choke off, nor was he aware of the heavy tread of someone moving in the adjoining room. All his attention was focused on what lay before him: Jenna's body, stark and still, lying exactly where he had last seen it. But with the face closed now. Empty. The tattoo faded to a pale blue mark on the pallid skin.

He did not go to her, did not kneel at her side. If anything, he drew back slightly, blocking the path of those who were pressing in from behind. There was a moment of confusion, people milling about in the

confined space, followed by a rumbling crash from the next room—
the whole house shuddering as the end wall collapsed under the impact of a tremendous blow.

"Don't let it escape!" Dorf yelled, charging into the swirling dust.

The villagers streamed after him, their weapons and their voices
raised threateningly, leaving Rabon alone in the dust-fogged room.

There was still a little light in there, from the remains of a brand
left smoldering in one corner. Enough light, at least, for him to see
the vague outline of Jenna's body. Enough, also, to reveal the look of
guilt and bitterest disappointment on his own face.

This, Jenna's death, was what he had most dreaded. And yet now
that it was a reality, he found it was bearable after all. In his heart, he
knew that if Dorf were to die, his sorrow would be much deeper.
Whereas now . . .

"I'm sorry," he murmured aloud.

It was all he had to offer—an apology. Not for failing to love her,
but for failing to love her enough. His present grief was not to be
compared with the heart-stirring misery of that wailing voice.

At the thought of that voice, his head jerked up. The distant clamor
told him that the hunt was still in progress; on impulse he left the
house, sprinted across the open space, and climbed the tower.

He was just in time. The bobbing cluster of burning brands told
him where to look: on the far side of the village. Where, by the feeble
moonlight, he saw a long blur of shadow move rapidly between the
furthest dwellings and pass effortlessly across the eastern wall.

Some minutes later, when Dorf and the other villagers returned,
he was waiting for them by the main gate.

"It's gone," Rabon told them. "I saw it jump the wall and head for
the swamp."

"What was it?" a man asked in an awed whisper.

"A shadowy thing. I'm not sure."

"Yes, but what was it doing here?" the man persisted.

"What did it want?" someone else added quickly.

Dorf, usually so patient with his fellow villagers, swung angrily
toward them. "Don't you have ears? Didn't you hear its sorrow? It

came to mourn Jenna's death. Whatever it was, its grief was no less than mine or . . ."

He was about to motion toward Rabon, but seeing the hard, dry-eyed expression on his son's face, he stopped abruptly. "Do you feel nothing?" he asked in a shocked voice.

Rabon shrugged uncomfortably, his blush of shame not apparent in the poor light from the few smoky flares. "I'm sorry she's dead, but . . . but . . ." He tried to explain his true feelings, and failed. "I hardly knew her," he finished lamely.

"Damn it, she was your mother!" Dorf burst out. "Does that mean nothing to you? Even that thing out there knows what it is to mourn! Are you less than that? Are you?"

Rabon winced under the attack, Dorf's accusations only adding to the guilt he already felt. "I . . . I can't help . . ." he stammered, struggling for words that refused to come. "I can't pretend . . ."

But Dorf, his shoulders hunched in sudden despair, had turned his back.

"I'll tell you what," one of the villagers confided to the crowd at large. "What happened tonight is only the beginning. If you ask me, something bad's on its way. And it'll be here sooner than you think."

Dorf nodded in agreement. "Yes, something bad," he muttered dejectedly. "And maybe it's already here. Maybe it's dwelt amongst us ever since . . ."

He fell abruptly silent, his voice under the strain of emotion. Almost furtively he glanced across at Rabon, as though dreading what he might find in his face. Then, with the same hunched attitude of despair, he shambled toward the candlelight still shining like a beacon at the window of his house.

Chapter Four
Sun Lord

They had just finished burying Jenna's body outside the walls when the sighting was made. All that could be seen at first, even from the tower, was a long column of dust far out near the western horizon, but later in the day a line of people emerged through the glare, the dust raised by their weary footsteps billowing out behind. As they drew closer, it became clear that they were not ordinary travelers: some were dressed in flowing robes of yellow and silver; others wore armor that flashed in the sun.

"Priests!" the villagers declared in amazed voices. "Guards! From the twin cities."

"Yes, but who leads them?" others asked doubtfully.

That too was soon apparent. The tall man at the head of the column wore a distinctive helmet of gold; in his right hand he carried a golden staff fashioned in the likeness of a viper. Another viper, this time a live one, was coiled tightly about his upper arm.

"The Sun Lord!" people began singing out. "Solmak is coming!"

Rabon, who had been deeply depressed by the events of the morning, was shaken by a surge of excitement as he watched from the tower. "She said one of them would come!" he broke out. "Jenna. She told me. And he has! He has!"

"Take care, boy," Dorf warned him, for he was already moving to the head of the ladder, eager to open the gate.

"Care?" He spun around to face the old gatekeeper. "Why? Solmak has come for me, like she promised. Don't you see?"

"I see only an armed column from the city of Tereu," Dorf growled. "What it's doing here we have yet to find out."

"You mean you're not going to let them in?" Rabon asked in a shrill voice, his cheeks suddenly flushed.

"Not until I'm sure of what they want."

"Well I'm sure!"

Before Dorf could stop him, he slid down the ladder and released the wheel. As he began turning it, grunting with the effort, the old man appeared at his side and placed a restraining hand on one of the heavy wooden spokes.

"Listen to reason for once," he cautioned him. "Let me challenge them while they're safely outside the wall. If they come in peace, all well and good. If not . . ."

But caught up in the excitement of the moment, Rabon was barely listening. All he could think of was that the fabled Sun Lord had crossed the desert to find him; that his natural father, previously only a name, was waiting on the far side of the gate.

"Let go!" he shouted, tugging at the wheel, trying to break Dorf's grip. When that failed, he pushed at the old man, catching him off balance. It took Dorf only a second or two to recover, but that was long enough for Rabon. Heaving at the wheel with all his might, he gave it another half turn, and the heavy gate, with a creaking of timbers, started to open, the afternoon wind whistling through the narrow gap.

This time Dorf did not bother to argue. Catching him up in both arms, he threw him down in the dust and pinned him there, both knees upon his chest.

"That's enough!" he panted. "Now get some sense into that head of yours. Out there stands the most powerful man in the land; a man—"

"No! Not just a man!" Rabon shouted, kicking and squirming in an effort to break free. "My father! D'you hear me? My father!"

Still the knees bore down on him, refusing to let him rise. And that was when he blurted it out: shrieking in anger something he did not for a moment believe; something he would ever afterward regret.

"That's what worries you, isn't it? The fact that he's my father and you're not. That's why you won't let me see him. Because . . ."

He did not have to go on. Dorf, his face bruised with pain, had scrambled hastily to his feet. It was all the opportunity Rabon needed. With the pressure gone from his chest, he was up in an instant, running for the gate, ignoring Dorf's shouted warning as he squirmed through the gap.

Behind him he heard the gate creak open; the rapid thud of Dorf's footsteps pursuing him across the sand. Up ahead were the people from Tereu. They had stopped about a hundred paces from the wall — Solmak at their head, his polished helmet glinting like fire in the late afternoon sunlight; the others, in their glittering armor or vividly colored robes, clustered around him.

Under normal circumstances, Rabon would easily have reached them first. Yet a sense of urgency must have been driving Dorf's aging body, because all at once Rabon was aware that the pursuing footsteps were bearing down upon him. He tried to speed up, his feet floundering on the loose surface. Already he had covered more than half the distance. Just one last effort and . . . but a groping hand had fastened about his collar, dragging him down; another hand pressed his face into the hot sand.

When he looked up, Dorf was standing above him, his feet planted protectively on either side of his body. Not more than a dozen paces away stood Solmak. At close quarters, he and his followers looked less splendid than they had: their armor and robes were caked with dust, their faces grimy and travel weary.

"Is this the way you usually greet guests?" Solmak asked, his handsome face creasing into a mocking smile.

"It depends what they've come here for," Dorf replied. "Whether they're friends or enemies."

Solmak's smile vanished. "Who are you to challenge my purpose here?" he asked in a haughty voice.

"Like you, I'm a gatekeeper," Dorf answered steadily. "It's my task to challenge anyone who approaches our village."

"Is it also your task to abandon your post?" Solmak sneered. "Or to leave the gate open while you chase a mere boy across the desert?" Behind him, some of his followers were beginning to laugh. "Tell me," he went on. "Who is this boy you chase? What makes him more important than your duty?"

Rabon was about to answer, but Dorf placed a foot on his neck and again forced his face into the sand.

"He's just an unruly apprentice, Lord," Dorf said, speaking far more humbly than before. "He was so excited at your arrival that he disobeyed me and opened the gate. I couldn't let that pass. I had to chastise him."

Solmak did not try to hide his disbelief. "And for this, an unruly apprentice, you left the village unprotected? Had you handed him to me, I would have chastised him for you. Gladly."

"There's no need for that, Lord," Dorf replied in the same humble tones. Quickly he hauled Rabon to his feet and made as if to drag him back to the village.

"Wait!" A single order, barked out, that stopped Dorf in his tracks. "If you're the gatekeeper, as you say you are, then you know all the comings and goings in this area. So cast your mind back some fourteen or fifteen years and tell me this: Did a woman called Jenna ever come here? A young woman she would have been, and a priestess, heavy with child."

"Yes—" Rabon began.

"No, Lord," Dorf broke in, speaking over him. "No woman of that name and description ever appeared at the gate."

Solmak glanced knowingly from one to the other. "There seems to be some disagreement between you."

As Rabon opened his mouth to speak again, Dorf slapped him hard on the face, silencing him.

"Pay no attention to him, Lord. He's a bit touched in the head and doesn't know what he's saying half the time. Why, he wasn't even born fifteen years ago."

A tall gray-haired priest, standing directly behind the Sun Lord, leaned forward and whispered in his ear. Solmak nodded and again looked directly at Dorf. "An apprentice you called him," he said incredulously. "And yet touched in the head! Are you asking me to believe you'd train a half-wit to guard your community?"

"Not a half-wit, Lord. A little affected by the moon, that's all. When the moon's near the full he . . ."

Before he could finish, Rabon tore himself free. "It's a lie!" he shouted. "It's all lies. A priestess called Jenna *did* come here." He pointed to a fresh mound of sand close to the village wall. "We . . . we . . ." He took a deep breath. "We buried her only this morning. Over there."

"And her child?" Solmak prompted him.

"I . . . I . . ."

"Go on."

"I'm that child."

He was watching the Sun Lord as he spoke, waiting for a quick look of recognition, even of pleasure, to light up his face. But Solmak's expression, already grim, only seemed to grow more forbidding—his cheeks becoming paler; his mouth stretched to a hard line.

"You?" The word more like an accusation than anything else.

"Yes, Lord. I'm her . . . her first-born."

"Aaah." The long drawn-out sigh of relief was peculiarly joyless. As joyless as the hard blue eyes—as brilliantly blue as Rabon's own—which continued to survey him.

"Jenna told me you would come," Rabon explained, lowering his head before that unfeeling gaze. "She said . . ."

Solmak dismissed his words with a contemptuous flick of the hand. Nodding to the two armed men close beside him, he grunted only: "Take him!"

Straight away they sprang forward, their long metal-tipped staffs held in the attack position.

"The boy's unarmed!" Dorf shouted.

His protest had no effect. The first of the men was already whirling his staff through a short, vicious arc that had Rabon stumbling backward. Again the staff whirled around, and this time Rabon staggered and fell, the metal tip fanning the hair on the top of his head. Now the man was towering over him, the booted feet thudding painfully into his side, the staff poised above his forehead, about to deliver a short stunning jab.

It was then that Dorf stepped in. He had drawn from his belt one of the heavy wooden pins used for wedging the great wheel of the gate. With this, he deflected the staff and then felled Rabon's attacker with a single round-armed swing.

"Run, boy, run!" he cried.

He pushed frantically at Rabon and turned, too late, to meet the second of the armed men. Before he could raise an arm in defense, he caught a glancing blow on the temple that knocked him sideways. He rolled over once and tried to rise, but the man was upon him—a metal knee-guard punching into his midriff, winding him badly; the clublike end of the staff raised for a final telling blow.

Except that Rabon had not run as Dorf had urged him to. His eyes blazing, the Sun Lord momentarily forgotten, he retrieved the staff of the fallen man and swung it fast and hard. There was a faint cry and the second man also crumpled over and lay still.

More of the guards were preparing to advance, plucking their staffs from the clips fastened to their backs, but once again the priest with the long gray hair was leaning over the Sun Lord's shoulder, whispering urgently to him.

"This must stop!" Solmak cried suddenly, holding both arms out sideways and pushing his men back. Then to Rabon, in a more friendly voice: "Drop the weapon, boy. No one will hurt you now. Believe me."

Rabon shook his head. Breathing heavily, from anger more than exertion, he stepped forward and placed himself between the Sun Lord and the old gatekeeper.

"Come, boy," Solmak said in gentle protest, and he too advanced, until he was only a pace or two away. "This is no way for us to act. Not people like you and me. We, more than anyone else, should trust each other. Isn't that so? Isn't it?"

It was a direct appeal. One Rabon yearned to respond to. For a moment he wavered and would have given in had it not been for

Solmak's eyes, still so hard and unloving, so little to be trusted in spite of his soft words.

"Why did you attack us?" he asked. "What did we do to deserve that?"

"Do? Why, nothing. It was a mistake, that's all. For which you have my deepest apology."

Once more Rabon gazed into those eyes, which were an older, mirror image of his own. What was it Jenna had told him of his father? "He won't fail you." Yes, that was it. "When the time comes, no matter how much you may hate or fear him, he'll be there." Yet how could he believe that while he was confronted by this face? The lines etched into the skin around the eyes and mouth were more than just a sign of middle age: they were also a mark of cruelty.

"No, not a mistake," he murmured unhappily, shaking his head. " 'Take him,' you said. I heard you."

"Yes, but I didn't mean you," Solmak protested. "I meant the old man. I thought he was threatening us. As for you and me, how could I possibly hurt you when we're . . . ?"

He broke off, acting as if his meaning were so clear to both of them that it didn't need to be stated. And beguiled by his tone, Rabon doubted his own instincts and relaxed. Only for a second, but still long enough for Solmak to dash the staff from his hands and catch him roughly by the hair, dragging him close against his armor-clad body.

"So, boy," he grated out, all his earlier gentleness vanishing, "you are Jenna's first-born. Is that right?"

Rabon, his face crushed into the molded armor-plate, could smell the stale sweat from Solmak's unwashed body. When he looked up, he could see only the shape of a helmeted head, black against the burning glare of the sun.

Nearby, there was a painful groan. "Leave him," he heard Dorf whisper hoarsely.

"Answer me, boy!" Solmak said in a threatening voice.

And when Rabon said nothing, Solmak tightened his grip on his hair and brought his other arm—the one bearing the coiled body of the live viper—close to his face.

Rabon, watching with terrified eyes, saw the tongue flick out and back, the small, deadly head draw in and gather itself, ready to strike. Only at the last possible instant was the creature jerked away, its gaping jaws, with fangs exposed, almost grazing his cheek.

"You may count that as a warning," Solmak said. "The only one you'll get. Now tell me the truth. Are you the child I'm looking for? Jenna's son?"

"Yes," he gasped out, flinching from the snake, which continued to regard him with its cold, diamond eyes. "I'm her first-born. I swear it."

"And the other child? The twin?"

"He's dead."

"You're sure of this?"

"The village cast him out hours after he was born."

"Aaah." The same joyless sigh as before. "Did you hear him, Pendar?" Addressing someone behind Rabon now. "Cast out only hours after birth. Just as you foretold."

"Journey's end, Lord," the priest answered.

"True, Pendar. Only this one still to deal with."

"No! Let him go!"

It was Dorf's voice; Dorf's powerful arms plucking Rabon free, away from the glittering snake-eyes, away from the sun-haloed head whose helmet flashed blindingly as it was buffeted aside.

Solmak's hand had relaxed its grip on Rabon's hair, and he and Dorf were running through the loose sand. Though only for a short distance. The illusion of freedom was shattered as Dorf pitched forward, a gaping wound on the back of his skull.

"Not the boy!" he heard Solmak cry.

And something jolted at him, a sudden sharp impact just behind his ear. He tried to keep running, his feet churning through the sand, uselessly; the low wall of the village, the half-open gate, somehow receding, disappearing into a deepening twilight. "Close it!" he tried to yell, at the faces watching from the tower—striving to will the gate shut with his dwindling strength. "Close it!" His mouth framed the words soundlessly even as the unnatural night enclosed him, blotting out the gate, the lingering image of Dorf's terrible wound, the last of the burning sunlight, everything . . .

Chapter Five
Flight

He awoke to true night and to a dull sense of pain. It was his head mainly, which hurt unbearably when he tried to stand up and walk. Also, there was something choking him, tightening about his neck and pulling him up short after only a pace or two. Crouched on the sand, he explored the darkness—his fingers detecting a rope that ran from his neck to a spoke on the great wheel of the gate. It was knotted just under his chin, but so tightly that he could not loosen it.

Held fast, he sank back wearily and gazed upward. Above him the sky was clear, dotted with stars, a waning moon casting inky shadows. One of those shadows appeared strangely broken. Or so he believed until he focused clearly and realized he was looking at what was left of the gate. There was a ragged hole in its heavy timbers where someone had battered at it; splintered sections of plank still littered the ground.

So they did close it, he thought hazily—remembering, as through a fog, how he had willed the watchers to protect the village. He began to remember other things too: the Sun Lord's eyes; the even colder eyes of the snake; the way he and Dorf had . . .

With a gasp he was on his feet. Fully alert, he noticed that candlelight was spilling from the door and window of his home. As was the sound of laughter.

"Dorf?" he called softly. And then louder: "Dorf?"

An armed figure appeared in the doorway and approached him. He could not see the man's face, only the cup of water being held out to him—which he took and gulped down.

"So you're awake," a voice said—a matter-of-fact kind of voice, not vicious or unfeeling.

"Dorf, where is he?" he asked.

"Dorf?"

"The old man who keeps the gate."

"Oh him. He's still lying outside. Pendar told me to finish him, but there didn't seem much point."

"Not much point?"

"Well, he's not likely to get up, is he? Not after a blow like that."

Again the tone was matter-of-fact, yet it brought home to Rabon a vivid image of Dorf stumbling forward, of the gaping wound that had suddenly appeared in his matted gray hair.

"So . . . so he's . . . ?"

"Dead?" the guard took him up. "As good as."

A faint whimper broke from Rabon, and he covered his face with his hands, his whole body starting to tremble.

Beside him, the guard stooped for the fallen cup. "I wouldn't waste too many tears on him if I were you," he said, not unkindly. "You'll need a few of them for yourself. It'll be your turn tomorrow."

Rabon, still dry-eyed, looked up at the dark outline of the guard's head. "Then what's the point of bringing me here?" he said bitterly. "Why didn't you finish us both out there?"

The guard chuckled. "It's not as easy as that. Not in your case. You're sort of special as far as I can make out. Anyway, Solmak's vowed not to have your blood on his hands. And Pendar agrees. He says it's a better idea to give you to the sun."

"The sun?"

"Yes, leave you in the desert without water, as a kind of sacrifice. Let the sun do its work. That's if the ants and vultures don't get you first."

"But why?" Rabon asked, almost as puzzled as he was horrified. "Why should Solmak want me dead?"

The guard gave another low chuckle. "You're asking the wrong man. I just obey orders. You'll have to put your questions to Solmak. Or Pendar. They're the ones who know what's going on." And with a cheery wave, he walked away.

Left to himself, Rabon withdrew to the shelter of the wall and crouched there, sleepless, as the moon climbed higher in the sky. From time to time he was shaken by uncontrollable bouts of shivering—caused not so much by the prospect of his own death as by the idea of Dorf lying outside the walls, injured and alone, with nobody to comfort him.

As the night advanced, that picture, of Dorf abandoned and possibly in pain, became confused with the throbbing pain in his own head. And also with another, similar picture: of Jenna, lying stretched out in her lonely room, her tattooed face lit by the smoky light from the reed torch.

"No," he whimpered, half asleep from sheer exhaustion. "No!" Vainly trying to fend off unseen hands—Dorf's, Jenna's—that were plucking at him; that refused to leave him in peace. One of the hands was gripping his shoulder with particular force, shaking him backward and forward; jerking at him so violently that his eyes flicked open onto the moonlit village.

And it wasn't a dream at all. Dorf was bending over him, urging him awake. The real live man, not some ghostly memory. He was also urging him to remain silent, one work-hardened hand closing over his mouth, muffling his cries of welcome.

"Quiet," he murmured, and nodded toward the candlelit doorway.

Stilling his joy, Rabon waited as Dorf cut the rope from his neck. Then hand-in-hand, they stole through the hole in the gate and out into the desert.

Once clear of the walls, Rabon could not restrain himself: tossing back his head, he let his relief and gladness break out in a loud peal of laughter. "The guard told me you were as good as dead," he explained, "I thought I was never going to . . ."

He stopped as Dorf stumbled and lurched against him. In the clear moonlight, Rabon saw with a sudden pang of concern that the aging face was almost as pale and gaunt as Jenna's, and when he threw both arms about the old man's neck, to prevent him falling, the sleeve of his tunic came away wet with blood. In an instant all his joy at being released, all his unspoken plans for stealing waterbags and trekking to the mountains, were forgotten.

"We must get you back to the village," he said. "You need help."

Dorf shrugged off his guiding hand, swaying slightly as he fought to keep his balance.

"No," he said, doggedly shaking his head. "We both die if we're found there. We have to hide somewhere." He raised his head and scanned the featureless plain, his eyes resting at last on the black shape of the swamp.

"Not there!" Rabon said quickly.

"Where else can we go? There's no other cover close by. And even if I wasn't injured, we'd never make it to the mountains. Solmak's guards would soon run us down."

"But the Night Lord's spirit!" Rabon objected. "It dwells in the swamp! I saw it going back there."

"Yes," Dorf said thoughtfully. "Jenna's 'familiar.' Hidden there all these years."

"If it caught us," Rabon whispered, "especially at night . . ." He shuddered at the prospect.

"You may be right," Dorf conceded. "Though there's this to consider: we've heard its voice; we know it has feelings. It can love and mourn like the rest of us. Who knows, it may also be capable of pity. Which is more than you can say of Solmak and that priest of his."

"But at night!" Rabon repeated. "Can't we at least wait till morning?"

Dorf never had to make that decision, for at that moment there was a cry from the village. It was soon echoed by other voices, a flare appearing at the hole in the gate.

"They've noticed you're missing," Dorf hissed, and began hobbling drunkenly across the sand.

Rabon caught up with him in a few strides. "Here," he said, and he took half the old man's weight on his shoulders.

For a while they kept up a reasonable pace—skirting the village in the shadow of the wall and heading straight across the irrigated fields. But as the minutes passed, Dorf's weight began to tell on Rabon, and gradually they slowed to a walk.

"We have to hurry!" Rabon insisted between gasping breaths.

For out there on the level fields, they were completely exposed; already the sounds of pursuit were growing louder.

Dorf, moaning with distress, slumped to his knees before one of the water channels. "It's no use," he protested, as Rabon dragged him through the muddy water and out onto the far verge. "I . . . I have to stop."

"A little farther, that's all," Rabon gasped. Dorf's full weight was on his shoulders now, his footsteps weaving an erratic path through a field of young corn.

They reached the next watercourse and waded across, but this time Rabon lacked the strength to haul the old man up the bank. Ahead lay the wide reaches of the pool, the descending moon perfectly reflected in its surface, and beyond the pool rose the somber shape of the swamp, a trackless region of twisted trees and stagnant, boggy ground. Looking at it now, Rabon was tempted to turn back; to face Solmak's judgment rather than enter what he had always been led to believe was a place of nightmare.

Behind them there were shouts of triumph, the cluster of flares bobbing crazily as their pursuers quickened their pace.

"They've spotted us!" Rabon cried, scrambling up the bank, pulling desperately at Dorf.

But the old gatekeeper made no effort to help him. "I'm finished," he murmured weakly. "You go on."

"Not without you."

"Go on, I say!" he tried to shout. "We'll both be taken if you stay."

Rabon sank down beside him. "How can I leave you here? How can you even ask that of me?"

"How? I'll tell you." Dorf had risen onto one elbow; his eyes, as he glanced hurriedly back, reflected the blobs of smoky light that were drawing nearer. "When Jenna gave you to me," he muttered, "she made me promise her something. That I'd always protect you. 'See to it that he survives and grows strong' — those were her instructions. 'Because there's a special purpose for him.' She said that too."

"Purpose?"

Dorf shook his head. "How should I know what it is? The ways of the twin cities have always been beyond me. But I promised her all the same. I gave her my word that no harm would befall you. That's why I'm telling you to leave. So I can keep my vow. Die with my conscience clear. Won't you help me do that? Is that too much to ask?"

"But Solmak may not kill us!" Rabon cried desperately. "Jenna said he wouldn't fail me. Not in the end. He may still . . . may still . . ."

"Come, boy," Dorf answered with a smile, and pointed to the lights, which had reached the far side of the field, their pursuers already splashing through the narrow channel. "Does that look like a rescue party? No, there's no mercy there. Not for either of us. So do as I say, make a run for it. Do that one last thing for me."

When Rabon still hesitated, the old man punched the ground with his clenched fist. "I'm begging you," he pleaded, "Isn't that enough? What more do you want? My curse? Is that what you're waiting for?"

"No!" Rabon protested, starting to back away.

But his voice was drowned out by the shouts of Solmak's men, who were almost upon them.

"My curse then!" Dorf screamed. "My curse on you!"

And with his hands covering his ears, Rabon began running, straining every muscle as he tried vainly to leave Dorf's final words behind.

He paused and looked back only once during his flight. Somehow, Dorf had managed to struggle to his feet, his bent body etched against the flares, his arms raised in defiance. Then he seemed to reel and spin as though responding to unseen music; arms other than his beating at the air; metal glinting dangerously as he slowly toppled and fell.

"Dorf!" Rabon sobbed aloud. "Dorf!" That one word keeping time with his pounding footsteps; the same word ringing out insistently as he splashed around the margins of the deep pool, the ripples caused by his rapid passage shattering the watchful image of the moon; no other word but that accompanying him to where the fields ended and a shadowland, far darker than all his imaginings, began.

Chapter Six
Swamp

He was brought to a halt by the touch of water, cold around his chest. He blinked, like someone waking suddenly, and looked around. He had blundered into a stagnant pool, its surface thick with foul-smelling scum, bubbles of even fouler-smelling gas rising from beneath his feet whenever he moved. Holding his breath, he waded through the slime and clambered up onto firmer ground. The blackened, tortured shape of a tree reared above him, its upflung branches filtering the moonlight that reached him only in scanty lacelike fragments. Straight ahead lay an even greater darkness: a jumble of twisted trunks and drooping vines, of gloomy waterlogged hollows, of insect cries that chirped on endlessly. Something thin and ghostly gray swirled toward him, making him start back, but it was only a patch of mist blown through the swamp by the night wind.

All his life he had feared this place, refused even to look at it when he had been sent to draw water from the deep pool. As a child, he had sat in the comforting dust of the village, in the glare of day, and listened to the old people's stories about it. How it was the dwelling place of the Night Lord's spirit, a thing so hideous and evil that the merest glimpse of its eyes was enough to drive anyone mad. One of those stories had struck him particularly. It described how a child had wandered into the swamp and been overtaken by darkness. All night long the villagers called her name, and one brave man actually went in after her. He was never heard of again. The next morning only the child emerged, though her parents wished she hadn't. She was deaf and blind, her eyes as silver and blank as the moon; and for the rest of her short life she talked only to Luan, her mad prattle and cackling laughter echoing through the village night after night.

That same story occurred to Rabon now, and he shivered and drew the neck of his tunic close. Yet much as he feared the swamp, still it cost him an effort to turn back, toward the open fields visible through the screen of trees. For what lay out there had become even more terrible to him: a familiar voice forever silent; a loved face he would never . . . never . . . But he shied away from the thought of so much emptiness, concentrating instead on what he could still hear and see.

Solmak's men had fanned out into an advancing line that had reached the edge of the swamp. As they clambered over logs and ducked beneath low-slung boughs, their flares jerked and swung like dancing lights connected by some invisible string. Voices continued to call, but anxiously now; that the faces appeared in the torchlight were wide-eyed with fear.

"How much further do you expect us to go?" Rabon heard a man protest.

"I say we turn back," someone else added loudly. "The morning will be soon enough for this kind of work."

One of the nearer flares probed the shadows, its flickering light reaching to where Rabon stood.

"Who . . . who's that?" a voice inquired fearfully.

Rabon stooped for a half-rotten branch and flung it as hard as he could.

There was a yelp of terror as the man turned and fled, his abandoned flare sizzling out in the damp undergrowth. The alarm spread quickly. Those closest to him cried out and flung their flares aside as they also ran for their lives; within seconds the whole search party was in a state of panic, scrambling back to the safety of the fields.

At any other time Rabon might have laughed, but not then. He gave only a grunt of satisfaction and was about to sink wearily to the ground when a very different kind of cry rang out. One that left him chilled and stiff with fright. It sounded again: a great roaring challenge, unearthly, that made the distant voices grow yet more shrill.

Rabon had whirled around and was gazing into the blackness of the swamp. Had the cry come from there? He wasn't sure. In among the trees it was hard to locate the source of any sound. Even the nearby hooting of an owl seemed to swirl and eddy through the thickly clustered branches, coming at him from several directions at once.

Slowly, as he partially recovered from his fright, he began backing away . . . and stopped. Where was he to go? Not back into the fields. He knew what awaited him there: a deathly stillness, a face as closed and empty as Jenna's. No. He was not ready for that yet. Forward then? Into the lightless depths of the swamp where, according to the villagers, the very ground quaked beneath your feet?

As if his secret thoughts had become part of the magic of this place, he suddenly felt the sodden ground on which he was standing give a violent shake. Once . . . twice . . . three times he felt it, the earth itself responding to unheard footsteps. He jerked his head from side to side, searching, but all he could see were the same twisted shapes of trees, the same filigree pattern of moonlight and shadow; the same miasma of mist drifting eerily through the confusion of vines and foliage.

"Luan?" he murmured, his voice faint with dread. "Luan, have you come for me?"

Again the ground shook, and he closed his eyes, his whole body clenched and waiting. Yet when, after a breathless pause, he dared to peek through trembling lashes, nothing had changed. The moonlight was as sparsely patterned as before; the bulky shapes of trees formed the same sinister circle all around him. Or was it quite the same? He peered more closely. The nearest tree was different from the way he remembered it. He even wondered whether it had been there at all. He shook his head in disbelief. And again, when he glanced back, the tree seemed to have moved, to have drawn closer, the ground responding to the movement with a faint vibration.

He wanted to turn and run . . . and couldn't. Almost directly overhead there was a high sound, soft, like a dawn wind lisping through the canopy. He looked up and saw two pale half-moons. Two! Eyes staring at him. A face hanging there in the gloom. So awful a face that he screamed and screamed again. A heavy branch swung down, became an arm and then a hand that reached for him, fingers that brushed against his head . . .

This time he ran, clawing his way through the darkness without thought or purpose. Loops of vine grazed his arms and legs; clammy strands of spider's web stuck to his bare flesh as he ducked and scrambled between trees; the spongy earth sucked at his feet, as though trying to draw him to itself. But still he ran on, crashing through the shrill silence of the swamp until, once again, he blundered into a pool—the crust of scum giving way beneath him; his weight carrying him under the surface, down into the mud and slime.

He came up spluttering, gasping for breath, and reached for an overhanging vine. It yielded slightly, but held, and he pulled himself clear . . . only to feel the vine twitch and move. Before he could let go, it had coiled itself around his hand, his arm. Thicker loops encircled his chest and began to tighten. In a jagged patch of moonlight, he saw it: another eye, diamond-clear and cold, watching him incuriously.

"Help!" he tried to scream, but the loops about his chest were crushing him, and only a faint murmur broke from his lips.

Already, as he fought for breath, there were streaks of bloody red obscuring his vision, a roaring in his ears that muffled all but the frantic beating of his heart. Even while he continued to struggle, he knew he was suffocating; he made a last desperate lunge at the watchful eye. But it merely drew further back, its diamond clarity reflecting the image of his groping fingers.

He had by then reached the edge of consciousness, his whole world threatening to sink into the void. Defeated, he was about to give himself to that void when something lifted him high and shook him.

He could feel his arms and legs jerking uselessly, like a puppet's. Yet amazingly, all that violence produced only a sweet sense of relief. The loops of cold muscle began to loosen their hold until finally they fell away altogether. And while he was still greedily sucking in air, he was lowered gently to the ground.

When he next looked up, the moon creature was hovering above him. Though now, having been saved by it, Rabon no longer felt terrified. He even looked into those half-moon eyes and thought he detected a hint of tenderness. Not that he found the face any less hideous. It had gaping black caverns for nostrils; a great gash for a mouth, the swollen tongue bulging from it; a snaggle of discolored teeth half embedded in bruised lips. As though uncomfortable beneath his gaze, the creature tipped its head away, and in a shaft of moonlight Rabon saw that its cheeks, its chin, its forehead, were dotted with wart-like swellings from which wiry black hairs sprouted. Similar coarse black hair covered its head and neck, falling in spidery drapes about horribly deformed ears—their outer edges bent and crumpled, the drooping lobes reaching almost to its shoulders.

"Who . . . who . . . ?" It made the same high sound Rabon had heard before, like wind through the trees, and with a start he realized that creature was speaking to him. "Name . . ." it added, the word, only just recognizable, lisping past the swollen tongue.

"Rabon," he answered.

"Ra . . . bon . . ." it repeated awkwardly. Then, pressing a vast hand to its chest, it said: "Lal . . . I . . . Lal . . ."

The exchange of names seemed to please it because it opened its mouth and gave a rumbling laugh. When Rabon failed to join in, it looked at him questioningly and reached down as if to touch his face.

Only then did Rabon notice the water snake, probably the same one that had attacked him minutes earlier. It was lying neatly curled around Lal's enormous arm, its head flattened against the back of the hand that was reaching for him. Hurriedly, he rolled clear and scrambled across the murky ground until his way was blocked by an ancient tree.

With his back set firmly against the knotted trunk, he peered nervously through the moon-speckled darkness, but the creature had not attempted to follow him. It too had squatted down and was facing him across the narrow clearing, its spread legs like low-hanging boughs.

"Rabon . . . Lal . . ." it breathed contentedly, and after heaving a deep sigh, it settled to sleep.

As the half-moons of its eyes blinked out, Rabon's first impulse was to sneak away. Silently, he half rose . . . hesitated . . . and finally sank back. For still the same question presented itself. Where was he to go? Not out into the fields. That remained unthinkable. It was better by far to stay where he was. Here at least he felt secure. No, more than just secure. The company of this creature, asleep only paces from where he crouched, actually comforted him. Hadn't it roared at Solmak's men? Saved him from the snake? The very snake that it now cradled lovingly. Oddly, that show of affection also comforted Rabon, making him feel doubly safe. And exhausted by all that had happened, he closed his eyes and joined his silent companion in sleep.

It was light, mist rising from the nearby pool, when he woke. He looked for the creature, but it was gone. Where? Had Luan perhaps recalled it? He had no idea.

Cautiously, he stood up. The snake, too, had disappeared; and the surrounding scene, which by night had seemed so black and forbidding, was utterly transformed. In contrast to his picture of it, the pool was covered by a film of brilliant green. A similar mossy green coated the trunks of the oldest trees; others were decorated with colonies of brightly colored lichen, the vivid oranges and reds gleaming like jewels in the dewy freshness of the morning. Other jewels showed among the vines and undergrowth — a whole host of blossoms opening themselves to the sunlight filtered dimly through the canopy. In that same dim light, spiders' webs glistened bright silver; the plumage of darting birds flashed yellow and gold — the air, the earth, the dark foliage of the trees, all teeming with life and movement.

For Rabon, accustomed to the dusty glare of the plain, it was a wondrous scene; he was still gazing in astonishment when there was a sound of heavy footsteps and the creature splashed through the pool toward him.

By day, it too looked slightly different: as hideously ugly as ever, and still with the water snake around its arm, but bigger than Rabon would have believed possible. The pool, which had closed over his head the night before, reached barely to the tops of its legs, and what legs they were! What arms! What massive hands and shoulders! Like the trees among which it lived, it was built on a colossal scale; its dark, hairy skin almost as gnarled and knotted as theirs.

It greeted Rabon with a high cry of welcome, and tipped a heap of freshly gathered food from the pockets of its rough tunic—brown-skinned mushrooms, scarlet berries, a collection of birds' eggs, succulent young shoots, and bulbs with the damp earth still clinging to them.

"Eat . . . eat . . ." It instructed him, pushing imaginary morsels into its gaping mouth.

Having eaten nothing since noon of the previous day, Rabon needed no urging, and although much of the food was strange to him, he devoured it hungrily, surprised at how tasty it was.

While he ate, the creature squatted nearby, its great black eyes watching his every movement, taking in every detail of his face. Once, it leaned forward and fingered his golden hair, unconcerned by the way Rabon cringed back.

"Sun . . . like sun . . ." it lisped, pointing up to the soft yellow light gilding the tops of the trees. And it laughed with pleasure, a rumbling sound that began deep in its chest and spread through the rest of its body, making it rock slowly from side to side.

Rabon forced himself to smile back. After all that the creature had done for him, he felt compelled to humor it; to treat it as he would a backward child. Yet as he had to admit, there was nothing backward about its behavior a few minutes later.

Not far from where they crouched, a freshwater spring bubbled up through the spreading roots of a tree, and once his hunger was satisfied, Rabon went to drink from it. As he stooped low, the bone charm given to him by Jenna fell from the front of his tunic and swung free.

With a crow of delight, the creature was upon him. Before Rabon could fend it off, it had grasped the charm with one hand and slipped the chain over his head with the other. After inspecting it carefully—especially the tiny clasp at one end—it produced a similar charm from the front of its own tunic. Then, with a quick, deft movement, it fitted the charms together. There was a faint click as the clasps meshed, and the next instant what had been two separate carvings had magically become one: a long flat piece of bone that showed two snake-heads, each with a jeweled eye, joined by the many twists and coils of a single body.

With another deft movement, the creature separated the charms and slipped Rabon's back over his head. It was looking at him strangely now, its mouth twitching with excitement. "Jenna . . ." it murmured joyfully. "Mother . . ." And it lunged forward and tried to embrace him.

He scrambled back out of reach, shaking his head in horrified denial, but the creature lunged at him again, catching him up in one hairy fist.

"Jenna . . ." it insisted, as joyfully as before. "Mother . . . mother . . ." Pointing first at Rabon and then at itself.

Rabon closed his eyes, as though trying to block out the truth that had dawned upon them both. Yet there was no denying it. The real identity of this creature, its monster-face now pressed lovingly against his own, was only too clear.

"Brother Night," he confessed through gritted teeth.

Chapter Seven
Return

Rabon and Lal ventured to the edge of the swamp only once on that first day. Lal led the way, gliding silently between the trees despite his great bulk, his huge feet somehow avoiding any twigs or fallen branches that might have betrayed his presence. By contrast, Rabon moved awkwardly over the uneven ground, snapping twigs or disturbing the undergrowth no matter how hard he tried not to. Twice Lal cautioned him, and when he continued to blunder on, the giant picked him up and carried him.

"Let go!" he cried indignantly, struggling helplessly in the powerful grasp. "Let me . . ."

His cry was choken off as his face was pushed gently but firmly against the coarse tunic.

"Did you hear that?" he heard someone ask in a whisper.

The pressure on the back of his neck eased, enabling him to peer through a cascade of vines and leaves. About twenty paces away, caught in a speckled patch of sunlight, were two of Solmak's guards. They were armed with the same staffs as before, except that now the metal tips had been replaced with spearheads. Both men were holding these spears straight out before them, their faces fearful as they gazed into the deeper shade.

"It must have been the boy," one of them replied in a trembling voice.

"So it has him! There *is* a night spirit in there, like the villagers say!"

As if to encourage this idea, Lal let out one of his deep roars — more muted than before, but still loud enough to send the two guards into a panic. Tumbling over each other, yelling a warning as they ran, they scrambled through the fringe of heavy growth and out into the sunlit fields.

Left behind in their flight, and now gleaming in the undergrowth, was one of the spears. Acting on the spur of the moment, Rabon squirmed free and ran to pick it up. He was back within seconds, flourishing the weapon triumphantly, but Lal shook his head and turned away, gesturing for Rabon to follow him deeper into the swamp.

They remained hidden for some days. From time to time they heard the guards calling to each other and occasionally they detected the more authoritative voices of Solmak and Pendar, but after the first morning, nobody ventured into the swamp. All the activity was restricted to the surrounding fields, and even that decreased as the days wore on.

Throughout that period of hiding and waiting, Rabon saw less of Lal than he would have expected. For whereas the giant slept most of the day, using the night to move quietly about his domain, Rabon remained watchful during the hours of daylight, glad enough to sleep away the long dark hours when the swamp was full of sinister sounds and shadows. The only occasions when they were truly together were dawn and dusk; those in-between times when night and day were balanced equally. Then, Lal would come and sit with him in the small clearing beside the pool, the water snake, as always, coiled around one arm.

"Brother . . ." he would lisp by way of greeting, and give a rumbling laugh as he pointed shyly at himself.

That word, which made Rabon shrink away, obviously gave him pleasure, because he usually repeated it during their brief encounters.

Apart from that he said very little, content to gaze at his companion with childlike curiosity.

Rabon tried to avoid that gaze as much as possible. Sullen and withdrawn, anxious about Dorf's fate, he often came close to hating the huge figure watching him through the shadows. Which was why it took him some time to understand Lal's silence; to detect, behind the ugly features and mild manner, a profound sadness.

He remembered then that Lal too was in mourning, for Jenna: the loving mother who had visited him daily, tending him in secret. Her loss had caused him to invade the village and howl out his misery. Although he had ceased to express his feelings in mournful cries, a real sense of grief clung to him still. So that once again, there in the deepening twilight of the swamp, Rabon felt guilty: accused of not caring enough for the mother he had hardly known.

Resentful at this comparison with his unlikely twin, he turned his back, biding his time until full darkness lured Lal away on his nightly ramble through the swamp.

There was nothing pointless about those rambles. Each morning, just before sunrise, he deposited freshly gathered food at Rabon's feet and then sat quietly nearby, watching as he satisfied his hunger.

One morning, however, he brought more than food. "Gone . . ." he cried, his voice high with excitement. "Gone . . ." Pointing in the direction of the fields.

Leaving the food uneaten, Rabon again accompanied him to the edge of the swamp, the two of them wending their way through the heavy mist. And sure enough Lal was right: when they reached the fields there was no trace of Solmak and his followers. All that remained to show they had been there were the trampled crops.

Glad to be free at last, Rabon made as if to step out into the open, but Lal lowered one arm, barring his way.

"Bad . . ." he cautioned him. "Nobody . . . comes . . . bad . . ."

There was no denying the sense of what he was saying: the absence of the villagers was a warning sign it would have been foolish to ignore. So for the rest of the day Rabon had to curb his impatience.

By evening still no one had appeared; unable to bear the delay any longer, Rabon collected his spear and prepared to leave. But again Lal tried to stop him.

"Stay . . ." he said, plucking gently at his sleeve.

When his hand was shrugged off, he shyly proffered some ripe berries. And all at once it dawned on Rabon that Lal was not just concerned for his safety: he was enticing him, persuading him to remain there as company.

"No," he said, shaking his head. "I have to go." Then, in a stiff awkward voice: "I wish to thank you for . . . for your help."

Dejected, his grotesque head drooping in disappointment, Lal stepped aside and allowed him to pass. Yet when Rabon glanced over his shoulder a few moments later, there he was, padding silently along behind.

"Get back," he cried. "I don't want you following me."

Lal's rubbery lips stretched into a sheepish grin, but he made no attempt to return.

"D'you hear me?" Rabon shouted. "You don't belong to me. That's your home, back there."

And he ran at the giant as though to spear him, but still Lal stood his ground, not even defending himself when the spear flashed threateningly before his face.

Planting one blunt finger on his hairy chest, he murmured, "Brother . . ." As though that one word were explanation enough.

As in a sense it was, for with a disgusted toss of the head, Rabon turned and ran on — conscious all the time of Lal striding along beside him.

The village was in darkness when they reached it, with nobody on the lookout tower and the damaged gate temporarily boarded up. Approaching the gate, Rabon peered between the boards. No light showed either from his house or Jenna's, which suggested that Solmak and his followers had in fact left.

"Dorf?" he called, hoping desperately that the old man had managed to survive.

The only answer was a howl of grief, which sent a shudder through his whole body. It was Lal, standing further along the wall, his face raised to the blackened sky. Even with the moon not yet risen, Rabon could see by the faint starlight what had torn that cry from him: a trampled area of sand where Jenna's grave had been; and a little further out into the desert, a scatter of whitened bones—all that was left of Jenna's body after being exposed to the vultures and other scavengers.

In spite of his earlier rejection of Lal, he would have gone and comforted him had he not noticed something else: the remains of another body, close to Jenna's.

With a sense of dread, he ran over. This body too had been re-duced to a skeleton. But whereas Jenna's corpse had been tossed naked onto the burning sand, here there were a few shredded remains of clothes: fragments of worn cloth that Rabon could not help but recognize, cloth that he had seen Dorf stitch and mend in the flickering candlelight. Nor was that all. Driven into the sand were four wooden pegs with leather thongs hanging from them—thongs that must have been tied to Dorf's ankles and wrists: his still living body pegged out in the hot sun to die.

"Solmak!" he whispered, mouthing the name as if it were a curse.

Only paces away, Lal continued to voice his grief, his wart-speckled cheeks wet with tears. Yet no tears pricked at Rabon's eyes: his cheeks not wet, but hot with rage. A rage that seemed to blaze with the fierceness of the sun, its white heat burning away any simple feelings of sadness.

Briefly, glancing across at Lal, it crossed his mind that perhaps he, Rabon, was the monster after all; that in spite of his hideous appear-ance, Lal was perhaps Jenna's true child. The one with the capacity to love and care. But how could that be? Lal had been fathered by Luan, a creature as mad as he was heartless. Everyone knew that. Whereas he was the son of the fabled Sun Lord. The guardian of light, of sanity. A man who had crossed the desert and . . . and done this! This! Who had brought with him, through the blinding heat of the day, only death and darkness. These poor stripped bones the results not of Luan's madness, but of Solmak's.

More hurt and confused than he could bear, Rabon clung to the only thing he was still sure of. His rage. His desire to avenge Dorf's death at any cost.

"Be quiet!" he snarled at Lal, and he lashed out with the blunt end of the spear, thwacking him cruelly upon the back and neck until his wailing cries had ceased.

Still in a rage, he strode to the gate and beat upon that. For several minutes the hammering blows echoed through the village. Then, at last, there was a light footstep on the tower ladder and someone peered furtively over the wall. Not a man or woman, as Rabon had expected, but a boy of his own age: the cooper's son.

"Who's that?" the boy called nervously.

"Rabon."

"You? But they said you were dead! That the Night Lord's 'familiar' had taken you."

"Well I'm alive, as you can see. And I'm looking for Solmak. Where is he?"

"He left yesterday evening, with his people. They've gone back to Tereu."

"Did they say why they'd come? Or why they were leaving?"

"Pendar, the priest, made a speech from this tower, but I didn't understand much of it."

"Tell me what he said anyway."

"That the two children were . . . were dead. So was the Moon Witch. And the brat's so-called father—those were *his* words. And how the Sun Lord still lived and—"

"Yes, yes," Rabon broke in impatiently. "But what point was he making?"

"I've told you, I'm not sure. Something about the old ways being dead. As dead as the sun child who would never keep the gate between the twin cities—I think he meant you then. He said something about the moon child too, and about the Night Lord being left to drown in his own dark waters, but none of it made much sense. The only thing he was clear about was Solmak. He told us that from now on he ruled the night as well as the day."

"Yes, the night," Rabon responded, nodding in bitter agreement. "That's what he's always been ruler of. Though not for much longer."

His closing threat was accompanied by another savage blow upon the gate, one of the makeshift planks splintering under the impact. Above him, the boy's face drew back in alarm.

"What can you do against Solmak?" he called down nervously. "What can anyone do? Look at what happened to Dorf when he tried to keep him out."

The mention of the old gatekeeper seemed to steady Rabon. "Listen," he called in a more restrained voice. "Bring me food, water. Enough to get me across the desert."

"But if you go after him, he'll kill you. He only left because he thinks you're dead."

"Maybe he'll be the one to die," Rabon replied.

He was conscious, even as he spoke, of how foolish he must sound—a poor village boy pitting himself against the Sun Lord. Yet for the moment he did not care.

"How can you kill Solmak?" the boy reasoned with him. "He's your father. That's what everyone here's saying."

Rabon's shoulders straightened with sudden resolution. His face, flushed until then, grew abruptly pale, as though reflecting the newly risen moon. "I have only one father," he answered deliberately, "and he lies dead on the sand behind me. I'm Dorf's son, no one else's. Remember that. Now bring me food and water. Or do I have to knock this gate down and get them myself?"

His determined tone must have convinced the boy because he disappeared. When he returned a few minutes later, the leather rucksack he lowered from the tower contained grain and a flask of water.

"There's one other thing," Rabon added. "A favor. Will you mind the gate while I'm away?"

"What . . . what if you don't return?"

The reality behind the question—his own possible death—made him pause before replying. "Then as Dorf's successor, I'm naming you. You'll become gatekeeper. The only one."

Saying that was like giving up a part of himself. But something still more testing awaited him. Steeling himself, he turned toward the two scattered heaps of bones—and noticed only then that Lal had disappeared. Strangely, that upset him, for he had wanted to say goodbye, perhaps even to thank the giant once again for saving him.

Shrugging off his disappointment, he marched over to where the four pegs jutted from the sand, tore them up, and began digging a hole with his bare hands.

It was hard work and took some time. Behind him, a sliver of moon rose steadily, casting his shadow on the shallow depression that gradually widened and deepened. He did not stop until his body was streaming with sweat and the sand lay heaped high on either side of a deep trough. Now came the most difficult part of all. Clenching his teeth, he gathered up Dorf's bones and placed them gently in the hole. Then, with feverish haste, as though trying to hide them not just from the vultures, but from memory as well, he pushed the sand back into place.

He was turning toward Jenna's remains, also intending to bury them, when Lal reappeared, his huge figure gliding silently along in the shadow of the wall. As Lal emerged into the moonlight, Rabon saw that he was no longer carrying the water snake. He had brought instead a sack made of woven rushes and a wooden club almost as big as a man, fashioned from the knotted root of a tree.

"There's nobody here to fight," Rabon told him, nodding toward the heavy club. "Solmak left yesterday."

But Lal's mind was not concerned with fighting. His eyes again brimming with tears, he dropped the club and slumped to his knees before Jenna's skeleton. With a tenderness and care that belied his size, he reached for the bones and placed them one by one in the sack. Only when the sack had been twisted closed and tied securely to his belt did he retrieve the club and stand up.

"City . . ." he said, and pointed off into the darkness. "Bury . . . Jenna . . ."

"Why there?" Rabon asked.

"Jenna belong . . . city . . . place to . . . bury . . ."

Although the words were disjointed, the meaning was obvious enough and once again Rabon was surprised by Lal's clarity of mind. On impulse, he reached out for the sack.

"Here," he said. "Give it to me. I'll take it to the city for you."

But Lal surprised him yet again. "Lal . . . take . . ." he insisted, pushing Rabon's hand gently away. "Lal walk . . . Lal bury . . ."

"It's a long way," Rabon explained, still hoping to dissuade him. "And you'll meet people who'll be frightened of you and treat you as an enemy."

Lal shook his head. "Friend . . . not enemy . . ."

"They won't know that. They'll try and stop you just the same. Maybe even kill you."

"Not kill . . ." He swung the heavy club onto his shoulder, as though in readiness. "People fight . . . Lal fight . . ."

And with those words, he strode out across the plain.

Chapter Eight
Sacrifice

For the next hour Rabon did everything he could to make Lal turn back. He tried threats, promises, flattery, and finally, in desperation, insults.

"Do you realize what you look like?" he jeered. "Why do you think Jenna hid you away? Because she didn't want to scare people with that face of yours. And here you are going to the city! What do you want to do, frighten people to death? Why can't you just stay in the swamp where your face won't do any harm?"

Lal stopped for the first time and stared down at him. "Lal . . . ugly . . . ?" he asked, surprised.

Rabon gave a mock shudder. "More than ugly. Horrible."

It never seemed to occur to Lal that he might question Rabon's judgment. "Lal . . . horrible . . ." he said, and again tears formed in his eyes, though now they were not being shed only for Jenna.

Seeing how crestfallen he was, Rabon relented, thinking he had done enough to send the giant back. "Not exactly horrible," he added quickly. "Different, that's all, from what people expect."

But having once put the idea of ugliness into Lal's head, he discovered it was firmly fixed there: as unshakable as the decision to bury

Jenna's bones in the city. "Different . . . horrible . . ." Lal murmured, snuffling unhappily to himself as he strode on.

Rabon gave up after that, settling to a steady trot that more or less matched Lal's normal walking speed. By day, it would have been a punishing pace, but in the cool of the night he was able to keep it up for some time. Not until early morning, the wafer of moon now hovering before him, did he start to fall behind.

"Stop," he gasped, his feet sinking ankle deep into the loose sand. "Let me rest . . . just for a while."

Reluctantly, Lal turned back and squatted beside him. "City . . . far . . ." he explained patiently. "Lal take . . . mother . . . you stay . . . village . . . wait for . . . Lal . . ."

"Me?" He did not understand at first. "Why should I stay behind? And wait for you?"

"One child . . . bury mother . . . one . . . not two . . ."

He realized then what he should have grasped all along: Lal thought they were going to the city for the same reason—to lay Jenna's bones to rest.

Tired though he was, he stood up and brandished the spear. "I'm not making the journey for Jenna's sake," he said harshly. "I'm following the Sun Lord, the man you saved me from. When I find him, it'll be his bones scattered on the sand."

Lal shook his head in disapproval. "Jenna say . . . no kill . . ." he said quietly, and he took the spear and snapped it across his knee. "No kill . . ." he repeated, tossing the pieces aside.

"What are you doing?" He could feel his former anger returning as he scrambled for the blunt-ended piece. Before he could reach it, Lal prodded at him with the club. It was the gentlest of nudges, intended only to deter him, but still it was enough to send him sprawling. Really angry now, he rolled over and grabbed at the spearhead lying nearby. Without thinking of the consequences, he hurled it straight at Lal, and would have found his mark had the club not been in the way—the metal point sinking deep into the knotted wood.

"I . . . I'm sorry," Rabon stammered, all his anger draining away. "I didn't mean . . ."

He dodged hastily aside as Lal advanced on him. But the giant had no intention of retaliating. Whatever else the attack had done, it had convinced Lal of Rabon's determination to seek out the Sun Lord. Plucking the spear from the club, he proffered it to his companion.

"Take . . ." he murmured dolefully. "For you . . . not for . . . Lal . . ." He patted the bulging sack at his waist. "Jenna . . . for Lal . . ."

It was not meant as a reprimand, but Rabon could not help feeling chastened. Lal's few lisped words had brought home to him the marked difference between their two journeys: one an errand of death, the other of mercy; hatred and love traveling side by side along a single path. For all he knew, Lal may have shared those same thoughts, because when they set out once again they were both far more subdued.

As though aware of Rabon's right to walk beside him, Lal governed his pace. And toward the end of the night he ignored his protests and hoisted him onto his broad shoulders, carrying him effortlessly over the rough terrain.

Dawn found them far out across the desert—the fields and swamp a dull green stain on the horizon. Up ahead the mountains rose through a haze of mist and cloud, their rocky face flushed pink. Gradually that pink faded as the sun reached over the horizon and flooded the plain with its hard light.

Still Lal walked on. Though as the temperature mounted, making the desert shimmer and dance, even his great strength began to fail. His footsteps became slower, heavier; his feet dragged wearily through the sand. Already, only a few hours after sunrise, the sky above them was flecked with gliding shapes: vultures, ever watchful, spiraling in the changing air currents.

"We have to find shade," Rabon muttered through swollen lips. The top of his head was unbearably hot, his mouth parched and sour.

Lal paused and gazed about him. In all that vast expanse there was only one obvious landmark—a khaki-colored shadow some two or three hundred paces away—and he stumbled toward it.

Close up, it became a grove of cactus, the fleshy trunks rising limbless, leafless, from the dry soil. Yet because they grew close together, they did offer some shelter from the sun.

Despite his weariness, Lal did not immediately sink down to rest.

After depositing Rabon in the shade, he borrowed the spear and used it to shear the spines from the nearest cactus. Plunging the weapon repeatedly into the greenish flesh, he made a gaping hole, which began to ooze moisture: glistening drops that were far more refreshing than the now warm water in Rabon's flask. For the next half hour they worked from plant to plant, until their thirst was slaked.

It was late afternoon, the sun glancing between the cacti, when Rabon woke. Lal was sitting a short distance away, but so preoccupied that he was not aware of being watched. He was holding the polished head of the spear up to the waning light, turning it this way and that as he tried to catch a glimpse of his own reflection. He must have been successful because he suddenly let out a groan and dropped the spear at his feet. Less certainly now, he picked it up and tilted it as before, only to drop it once again, snatching his hands away as though it were hot, his head rearing back from the ogre-face that had peered out at him.

Rabon went over and tucked the spear into his belt, where it could do no further harm. He would have liked to offer words of comfort, but could think of none. The terrible reality of Lal's face rendered all comfort useless, or so he believed as he pointedly turned his back and opened the rucksack.

Yet Lal, for some reason could not let the moment pass without comment. "Lal . . . horrible . . ." he lisped, repeating the words he had used the night before, but adding: "Rabon . . . beau . . . beau . . ." The word was too much for him, and he said instead, his voice totally free of envy: "Good . . . Rabon good . . ."

"No." In a moment of honesty, Rabon rejected the idea, the precious grains spilling unnoticed from his hands. "Not good."

"Yes . . . good . . ." Lal insisted, waving aside Rabon's protests as he stooped to gather up the fallen grain.

The sun was down when they finished their meager meal and turned their footsteps toward the mountains. In the cool of the waning dusk they walked the shadowless side; thereafter they used the stars to plot a westerly course.

Before the night was half over, Lal had again lifted Rabon to his shoulders, and with no one to slow him down, he strode out strongly, his long legs carrying them toward the mountains faster than a man could run. By the time the first gray hint of dawn was dimming the stars, they were into the foothills—a series of sharp ridges and deep gullies eroded not by water, but by wind.

That wind was blowing now, whistling past them in fierce gusts that threw sand up into their faces.

Unlike their actions the previous morning, this morning Lal was the one who decided to stop. With the sky lightening above them, he pointed toward a shallow cave in the side of a nearby gully.

"No, not yet," Rabon objected, urging him on. "We can keep going for a while longer. Till it gets hot."

Lal shook his head doubtfully. "People . . . watch . . ." he said, his dark eyes surveying the surrounding hills. "See Rabon . . . see Lal . . ."

"What if they do?" he answered carelessly, so eager to press on that he forgot what he had been told about the mountain folk.

But not Lal. Reared in the more testing world of the swamp, where he had constantly to hide and watch, he remained suspicious. "Face . . ." he said, and touched his own forehead. "Different . . . enemy . . . not friend . . ."

They were Rabon's own words—the very warning he had sounded outside the village. A warning he now chose to ignore, spurred on by the hope of catching up with Solmak.

"What are you worrying about?" he sneered, slipping down from Lal's shoulders. "How can you be treated as an enemy if there's no one here?"

He was already walking on ahead, as if to demonstrate the emptiness of the foothills, when he caught a flicker of movement from the corner of one eye. He spun around . . . and saw nothing. The flanking ridges were empty; the gray-edged shadows of early morning undisturbed by the regular gusts of wind. He half suspected then that he should have taken Lal's advice, but stubbornly he clung to the idea of not wasting this cool time of day. He detected another movement, on the opposite ridge . . . and again, when he looked, he saw nothing. There was only the wind sighing past, tugging at his hair, his clothes; the raised dust swirling like eddies of mist in the uncertain light. Behind him he heard Lal's growl of complaint, and still he plunged on: laboring across a bare slab of rock and down into a deserted gully; up again, over a slanting ridge, to be confronted by a gully as deserted as the last.

The light was strengthening now, the top edge of the sun winking over the horizon. Its presence gave to the rough terrain a harder, sharper quality, which accentuated the emptiness. And for a while Rabon decided that he was right after all. There was no one here to slow their progress. Those suggestions of movement, of someone spying on them, had been tricks of the light, specks of blown dust troubling his vision. He glanced back, to where Lal was moving more warily up the slope, and wanted to laugh, to call out encouragement, but the slope was too steep and he needed all his breath just to keep going.

Topping another of the slanting ridges, he slid down into a particularly narrow gully, steep-sided and deep. Up ahead, it ended in a jumble of boulders, some so big that the spaces between them were like dark caves. The sun was growing hotter by the minute, despite the blustery wind, and he thought: There, that's the place to stop. He even turned toward Lal, to tell him he had found them shelter for the day.

That was why the first real inkling of danger was signaled by Lal's raised face, his tongue pushed out past his snaggle of teeth as he bellowed a warning. At almost the same instant there was an ominous rumbling; when Rabon turned back, the top of the gully was somehow different. One of the caves was bigger, wider—growing wider still even as he watched. He wondered for a moment whether perhaps the whole hillside was splitting in two, for the ground was trembling, the grinding of rock against rock becoming louder. Then, with a rush, he recognized what was happening: several of the boulders at the top of the gully were jostling together, one of them tearing loose and rolling toward him, gathering speed alarmingly.

Lal reacted more quickly than he. "Go!" he roared. And when Rabon failed to respond, he pushed past him, placing his own body directly in the path of the advancing boulder.

It was hurtling along by then: filling the whole gully; flattening everything before it; leaving a boiling cloud of dust in its wake.

Rabon leaped for the side of the gully, scrambling for hand- and footholds, but the loose shale slipped beneath his fingers, sending him crashing down. He did not need to look: the boulder was right there, above him. Cringing away, he buried his head in both arms and heard the impact of rock upon flesh, heard the creak of Lal's sinews as he took the full force of the boulder and resisted it, heard the explosive grunt as the air was forced from his lungs. Dust followed, a wild storm of it billowing around them. As it cleared, he looked up and saw Lal's hazy outline: his body braced beneath the weight of the boulder still clutched in his arms.

"Go!" he groaned, not attempting to move, for the rumbling had started again. Another of the boulders had detached itself and was rolling toward them.

Rabon was only halfway up the gully when it struck. Had it reached him, he would have been swept to his death—another helpless speck of dust in the swirling cloud of destruction. But Lal was still there, blocking the way. Straining forward, he heaved the first boulder at the second. The two mighty stones smashed together, splintering into heavy fragments that rained down upon him.

Once again Lal was engulfed in a cloud of dust; again, when the dust cleared, he was standing his ground. Though now he was swaying like a tall tower about to fall, his feet and the lower part of his legs buried in a tumble of shattered rock.

"Go!" he groaned, for the third time.

And Rabon clawed his way to safety as another of the boulders rumbled down the slope.

It struck with the same ferocity as the others. Even so, it seemed for a moment as though Lal might resist it. With a challenging cry, he flung himself forward, taking the impact full on his chest, both arms pushing outward and up. For a split second he and the boulder remained locked together, two equal forces poised in conflict. Then he was falling backward, one leg crumpling under the strain, his hands buffeted aside, and in a churning cloud of dust and stones, he was swept away, his body turning over and over as he was carried down the gully.

"Lal!" Rabon shrieked—running, slithering, scrambling along the downward slope of the ridge.

Far below him the avalanche had stopped at last, though he could see nothing through the pull of the dust. The wind moaned aloud, a series of heavy gusts driving the dust away. And he saw it then—a truth he would rather have been spared. Lal, half-buried under a mass of debris: his face closed and bruised; his flesh torn and bleeding; his limbs and body deathly still.

"Hold on!" he shrieked uselessly. "I'm coming!"

But he wasn't. Again there were flickers of movement, to his left and right, and scurrying forms ran at him from several directions. He dodged, but they were too quick. A sinewy hand grasped at his ankle, bringing him down. He shook it off and tried to rise, only to be grabbed by other hands. Small arms and legs, wiry bodies, pinned him down; pallid, grinning faces pressed against his.

"Lal!" he wailed. "Lal!"

There was no answer, his cry snatched away by the wind. While Lal, far more helpless than he, lay bloody and unmoving in the gathering heat of the day.

Chapter Nine
Captive

With his hands tied securely behind his back, he was led forcibly along the narrow ridges and gullies and up through the even narrower passes, prodded on by the stone-tipped weapons of his captors. To begin with, he took every opportunity to look back, in the vain hope that he would see some faint stirring among the rocks and debris where Lal lay. But the only signs of movement were the swathes of dust blown by the wind, and soon he was too far away to distinguish one gully from another.

Still in a state of shock, and more dejected than he dared admit, he was given no chance to stop and grieve. Always he was hurried on, and no matter how fast he went, still his captors expected him to go faster—for the steepness of the climb, which left him dizzy with breathlessness, had no effect on the men and women who swarmed around him.

They were wiry figures, amazingly small, with pale round faces and dark eyes. "No stopping!" they shrilled whenever he stumbled. "Boran says no stopping!" And they would goad him with their spears until he broke into a gasping run.

He hardly remembered most of that day. Too tired to raise his head, he was aware only of the shaly rock passing beneath his feet, of the fine dust that caked his nose and mouth and often choked him, of the wind that grew stronger, cooler, as they mounted higher.

That evening he barely had energy enough to swallow a few mouthfuls of food before he fell asleep—a deep dreamless sleep from which he emerged shivering with cold.

The night by then was half over, the stars drawn into bright clusters that glittered icily. Some of that iciness had crept into his bones, and his cry for help came out in a series of broken whimpers.

A woman crawled over and stared down at him with hard button eyes.

"Fr-eez-ing," he managed to stammer.

She seemed puzzled at first, as though the idea of being cold were foreign to her—her own lean body even more scantily clad than his. Only when she touched him, felt how chilled he really was, did she understand. Then she shrugged helplessly, holding out empty hands to show she had no warm covering to offer.

"Pl-ea-se," he insisted.

She moved off, and moments later the sound of voices reached him.

"It's the only way," he heard the woman say firmly.

"But he's not of our flesh," a man replied. "Look at his skin and hair. He's a thing of the sun, of the hot plains. Why not let the mountains put their mark upon him?"

"You know why not. Boran told us to keep at least one of them alive."

"What if he did? There's no sense in such an order. The boy has to die soon anyway."

"Yes, but only after Boran has seen him. He has to be sure this is the child."

"The boy's head would be enough for that. There's no need for the rest of him, alive or dead."

The woman's voice rang out sharply in the crystal air. "If you're so eager to sever heads, why did you leave the monster's head attached to its body? Why didn't you bring that too?"

There was an uncomfortable pause. "Would *you* have touched a thing like that?" the man replied at last. "I wasn't the only one scared to go near it. But the boy's different. One stroke of the axe and—"

"Take care!" the woman broke in, her tone openly threatening now. "Boran is still the keeper, not you. If you act hastily, he may decide to deliver more than just the boy's head to the Sun Lord. He may carry yours through the Mountain Gate as well."

The argument petered out after that, and soon she was back with her companions. Silently, not trying to hide their distaste, they gathered about Rabon and pressed their warm bodies against his. For a while he continued to shiver, feeling nothing; then their combined heat had its effect and, gratefully, he slept.

The next morning dawned clear, but within an hour their upward journey carried them into a region of fierce winds and swirling mist. As he had learned from Dorf, this was truly the home of the mountain folk: a place so shrouded by cloud that the sun and moon were rarely seen; a place where only the craggy peaks were held in reverence. To Rabon, such harsh surroundings looked bleak and unlovely, far uglier than the sun-dried plain on which he had grown up. Clearly his captors reacted differently, the tearing winds that howled through the passes brought only smiles to their pale faces and the chill touch of mist made them call happily to each other.

Miserable and cold, with frost clinging to his eyelashes and hair, Rabon stumbled on. Up yet another pass where long stalactites of ice hummed in the wind; out onto a raw exposed slope, the powdery snow gusting into his face; and into a narrow valley, sheer-sided, which cut a clean path between towering peaks. Right across this valley the mountain people had built a massive wall of stone—as craggy and forbidding, as impassable, as the peaks that rose abruptly on either side. Set into the base of the wall, and offering to travelers the only possible route through the mountains, was a heavy wooden gate studded with nobs of steel.

As Rabon and his captors drew closer, the guards in the lookout posts called out a greeting. Immediately, other people began to appear, hurrying eagerly from caves cut into the sheer sides of the valley. There were many such caves: some at ground level, others with rocky steps leading up to them; from each of their dark mouths shreds of what Rabon took to be mist were drifting out into the gray windy day. He only realized his mistake when he pushed through one of the openings and felt the sticky warmth of steam on his skin.

He found he was standing in a wide, low-ceilinged chamber lit by several oil lamps. The lamps were burning brightly, yet in spite of that the light in there was strangely dim, made fuzzy by tendrils of steam that drifted up from the surface of a pool set into the rocky floor. The pool itself, quite small and obviously fed from below by a hot spring, was bubbling gently. Beyond the pool, indistinct in the steamy atmosphere, stood a man. He stepped forward, and Rabon saw that he was slightly taller than most of the mountain folk; his eyes darker, harder; his beard, the hair on his head, on his bare arms, much thicker and blacker than on any of his fellows.

"Yes," he murmured, surveying Rabon carefully, "this is one of them. There's no mistake." He switched his attention to the woman standing at Rabon's shoulder. "What about the other one? The monster child? Is that still alive?"

"There was a giant with him, Boran. A huge thing, that we had to kill."

"But definitely a monster?"

"Yes."

"And traveling in which direction?"

"Towards the setting sun."

He pulled thoughtfully at his dense growth of beard. "So the Sun Lord was wrong," he muttered half to himself. "They did survive. Both of them dogging his footsteps back towards the west just when he thought he was secure. Now that's an interesting turn of events." Again he fixed his eyes on Rabon. "Tell me, boy," he said coolly, "why were you following the Sun Lord?"

Rabon, who had begun to recover from the cold, made an attempt to sound defiant, unafraid: "Why shouldn't I follow him?"

Boran responded by breaking into noisy laughter. "Just listen to the boy," he said, wiping tears from his eyes with one hairy hand.

"I asked you a question," Rabon insisted, clinging to his air of defiance.

Boran stopped laughing and eyed him critically. "I'll tell you why not," he answered. "Because sane people don't seek their own death. Good or bad, high or low, we all try and save our skins."

"All except Lal," Rabon muttered in an undertone.

He had not wanted to say that. Or even to think it. The words seemed to emerge of their own accord, from some secret part of himself that would not be silenced.

"Except who?" Boran asked, cupping a hand around one ear.

Rabon shook his head. "Someone you don't know," he said unhappily. "Who didn't care enough about himself to . . . No, that's not right. It's just that he cared about other things more."

"Then he's a fool. And you are too. For not having the sense to run away from your worst enemy."

"But why is Solmak my enemy?" Rabon asked, hoping for an answer to the question that had plagued him for days.

Boran gave him a disbelieving look. "Don't play the clown with me, child. Why indeed! Because like any sensible leader, he fears his successor, the one who would strip him of his power. His only real defense is to seek your destruction before you reach manhood. What else would you have him do? Don the garments of humility and submit to you? Let the key to the Sun Gate slip freely through his fingers? No, that is not how the world works. For all his faults, Solmak is a man after my own heart. He knows that when it comes to the point, it's his head or yours."

"Then it will be *his*," Rabon said grimly—remembering at that moment not only Jenna and Dorf, but also Lal, standing bravely in the gully.

Boran greeted his answer with another burst of laughter. "Ah, what it is to be young and hopeful," he said merrily. "Though time will soon change that. A very short time in your case. Just as long as it takes for an axe to fall." He let one hand slice down upon the other in a rapid chopping motion. "The passage from youth to age, from hope to despair, all crammed into the space of a single breath. How does that sound, boy?"

"What . . . what do you mean?" Rabon asked nervously.

But he had already guessed, for Boran had moved to the side wall and lifted down a large stone-headed axe.

"Mean?" he said with a mocking smile. "I mean that your head is about to part company with your body. What else?"

Although he continued to smile, there was a sinister ring to his voice that made Rabon cringe inwardly. He struggled to return the smile, to appear unconcerned, but his nerve failed.

"I don't understand!" he burst out. "Why should *you* want to kill me? We've never seen each other before!"

"And never will again," Boran said in the same playful tone, and he ran his thumb lightly along the sharpened edge. "As to the why of it all, surely you can guess. Alive, you're a threat to Solmak and worthless to me. Whereas that head of yours is worth a head of gold in Tereu."

Before Rabon could attempt to answer, hands gripped him from behind, forced him to his knees and pressed his head down onto the stone ledge surrounding the pool. The rising steam made his eyes water, and through a film of tears he watched Boran's legs step slowly around the pool toward him.

"Wait!" he cried desperately, prepared to say anything in order to delay what was about to happen. "If . . . if it's gold you want, then . . . then I'll pay you more than Solmak. Much more!"

"More? How can a boy like you outbid the Sun Lord?"

Rabon's mind raced frantically as he sensed the axe being lifted. What did he have to offer that Solmak could not double, treble? His mind went momentarily blank, and then cleared. Somehow he managed to work one hand free—his fingers clawing at the chain around his neck, dragging the charm out from inside his tunic. "Here!" he shrilled, his voice on the edge of hysteria. "Take it!"

As he held it up, the jeweled eye of the snake caught the lamplight and gleamed briefly.

"What's this?" Boran asked. He had grounded the axe and stepped forward to a closer view. "What are you doing with this charm, boy?" he demanded suspiciously. "Did you steal if from the monster child? Is that how you came by it?"

"No," Rabon answered, his head still pressed firmly onto the ledge. "He had one like it, but this is mine. Given to me by my mother. As a

. . . a guide for . . . for when I'm lost . . . to show me the way where . . . where the sun can't reach."

They were mainly Jenna's words, not his, which he remembered from their last meeting. Words that meant little to him, that he blurted out now simply because he could think of nothing else to say. Yet to his relief they had the desired effect, for at a signal from Boran he was released and allowed to stand.

To his surprise, Boran was gazing at him with a new respect. "You may be a fool, boy," he said admiringly, "but at least you're a brave one. To go looking for Solmak would be dangerous enough. But Luan! And what for? His help? His protection?" He shook his head. "Luan is a monster of the night. A creature so debased that he destroys even his own young. All we can do is appease him, hold him at bay by satisfying his hunger. This is the first duty of the Sun Lord. Surely you, above all, must realize that. As for wanting to seek him out, to enter his forbidden realm . . . Follow that path and it will lead you only to madness and despair. Or worse. What possessed you to consider the idea?"

Rabon—bewildered by what Boran was saying, amazed at finding himself alive—hardly knew how to answer. "What . . . what other path is there?" he said vaguely.

"For someone in your position, I suppose that's true," Boran conceded. "But to decide to venture in there! Where only the dark water and its creatures hold sway. Why do you think the Sun Gate is always locked? Why does Solmak, for all his pride, pay a monthly tribute? It would be bad enough were Luan to grow dissatisfied and break out. But to choose to face him on his own ground! Most of your kind would rather die than . . ."

Confused by everything else Boran was telling him, he grasped quickly at the reference to death. "You say I'm going to die anyway," he cut in, hoping for a denial.

Boran gave a helpless shrug. "I can't alter the way things are," he said apologetically. "The gold and supplies I'll get in exchange for your head are too tempting to refuse. But because I admire bravery, I'll do this much for you. I'll deliver you to the city alive. As for the rest, it's up to Solmak. He can do his own dirty work."

Unsure what was expected of him, Rabon nodded his head in thanks.

"In the meantime," Boran went on, "get some food and rest. We'll set out tomorrow at dawn."

He waved Rabon away, but then, as an afterthought, called him back. "A word of warning, my young friend," he said in a low voice. "Don't mistake my generosity for weakness. If you do, your head may yet leave here on the point of my spear."

With that threat to accompany him, Rabon was led out into the windy valley, the rush of cold air making him shiver and hunch forward. Dog-tired now, he followed his captors up a flight of steps and into a much smaller cave. It had no boiling pool of its own, only a vent in the floor through which steam rose from below—the trickle of warmth just sufficient to take the deep chill from the air. Here, he was given a bowl of broth and a portion of cooked meat and then left alone. After his years of living on vegetables and grains, he had to force down the meat. Yet it did help to warm him, as did the goat-skin rug he found in one corner and wrapped around his shoulders.

He had intended to rest only for a short time but the grueling march through the mountains had taken its toll, and when he next opened his eyes it was evening. The unlit cave was almost dark, the narrow entrance no more than a dusky oval.

For a few minutes he lay there warm and comfortable, thinking back over his conversation with Boran. Although it had left him as mystified as ever, one thing at least was clear. He had gained a re-prieve; he was to be delivered alive to his enemy. There were, he admitted grudgingly, certain advantages in going along with that plan. He would be sure of reaching the city and confronting Solmak with his crimes. Also, during the journey he would be able to find out why his own father hated and feared him so much. On the other hand he would be a prisoner. Powerless. Delivering himself into the hands of a man who had shown neither pity nor mercy.

Shaking his head in silent rejection of that prospect, he eased aside the goatskin covering and crept to the open doorway. A single guard, his back to the cave, was standing outside. He was a small, slight figure even by the standards of the mountain folk. Someone Rabon could perhaps overcome if . . .

He did not give himself time to consider the consequences. Silently, he collected the goatskin from the corner. Holding it like a net, he leaped out upon his guard and threw it over the man's head and shoulders, dragging the startled figure back through the entrance before his muffled cries could reach those below.

There followed a violent struggle. The guard, far stronger than he had expected, fought and kicked. All Rabon could do was hold on as they thrashed wildly from side to side. Soon his arms were aching unbearably, his shoulders and back bruised from crashing into the wall. With one last effort, he drove forward, landing heavily on the man as they hit the floor together. And all at once the fight was over; the guard, when Rabon stripped back the skin, was lying there unconscious.

Badly winded himself, Rabon staggered to the doorway and looked out into the falling dusk. What he saw made his heart sink. The gate was still open, but there was a great deal of activity all around it. Flares were burning raggedly from the lookout posts on top of the wall; storm lanterns were bobbing around as the inhabitants of the caves bustled backward and forward across the valley. So many people to spot him as he stole through the failing light! So many people to pass when even one small guard had tested him to the limit!

Faced with the difficulty of his task, he hesitated. Stood there irresolute. Allowed himself, for the first time since his capture, to think consciously about Lal. Not just with regret, but with longing. A strange kind of longing, for the reassurance of the giant's courage and strength, and for something else too. Something lacking in his own vengeful journey. In himself. Which he . . .

Unbidden, the image of Lal standing steadfastly in the gully rose into his mind. With a sobbing cry, he tried to blot it out. But his own wild thoughts refused to be banished. They even threatened to invade the world around him. For when he glanced down, one of the bobbing lanterns seemed to throw out a familiar shadow: of a giant figure striding across the valley. He knew it was an impossibility, a trick of the light, his own imagination making him see things that could no longer be. Though still he yearned for it to be true. And he searched hungrily, uselessly, among the many lanterns for another such shadow.

What recalled him to the present was the groaning of the guard. It reminded him that any real chance of escape was rapidly slipping away. Within minutes the alarm would be sounded, and the activity around the gate suggested it was on the point of closing.

Stepping out into the icy wind, he picked up the guard's fallen staff and padded quietly down the stone steps. On either side of him the valley rose sheer, the upper levels lost in darkness. Wind-blown fragments of cloud were swirling over the wall, half obliterating the flares burning above the lookout posts. Under cover of a thick patch of cloud, the flares reduced to reddish sparks, he made a run for the gate.

At every step he expected to be challenged . . . and wasn't. The lanterns, the shadowy forms—like the mist and cloud—floated rapidly past him; the roar of the wind drowned out his pounding footsteps, his gasping breath. Directly ahead, he could see a group of people pushing at the massive gate, slowly easing it closed. So slowly that with a surge of excitement he realized he would reach it in time; slip through the gap and away, out into the safety of the night.

He quickened his pace and was almost there when the challenge came.

"It's the boy! Stop him!"

A man rose up in his path and Rabon struck at him with the staff. Another took his place, and frantically he wrestled him aside. But now the wind, rather than the mountain folk, was his enemy; shrieking through the narrowing gap, it buffeted him backward; like a live opponent, it made him fight for every step. Head down, his hair streaming out behind, his tunic almost torn from his body, he strained forward, groping for the great post beside the gate. Had he reached it, he could have pulled himself through; but a spear, thrown from above, thudded between his feet, delaying him. He wrenched it from the rocky soil and leaned again into a wind that abruptly slackened as the gate, with a shuddering of heavy timbers, locking into its frame.

In the brief lull, he turned to face his pursuers. They were all around him: faces, weapons, shimmering lanterns, ringing him in. With the staff whirling above his head, he tried to beat them away. A few fell back, but others took their place. More were tumbling from the caves, their lanterns, swinging wildly, throwing long shadows across the valley. Shadows so huge and grotesque, so hauntingly familiar, that he was tempted to believe that the impossible could happen; that what he had glimpsed minutes earlier had been more than an illusion. Lal, like the moon spirit, able to break the bonds of darkness and death. To rise again through the night.

"Lal!" he wanted to scream—much as he had screamed his name beside the silent gully. And with the same result. For when the crowd parted and the lanterns settled into stillness, it was only Boran who advanced through the gloom, his pallid face heavy with anger.

Chapter Ten
Hostage

"So this is how you repay my generosity," Boran cried, shouting above the roar of the night wind. "I offer you a few more days of life, and you take me for a fool. Well I won't make that mistake twice. Your head, Solmak asked for. And your head he'll get!"

He was standing in the pale glare of the lanterns, his dark eyes tinged yellow-red, his thick-set body bunched with fury.

Rabon, surrounded now by armed men and women, had dropped the staff. "What did you expect me to do?" he protested. "Give myself up without a struggle?"

"Expect?" Boran echoed him angrily, and snatching a spear from one of his followers, he pressed its point against Rabon's neck; the sharpened stone puncturing the flesh so a drop of blood ran down his chest. "Twice your life has been spared by me or my people. Twice! Once in the gully when the monster was killed; again when I chose to leave my axe unbloodied. Does that deserve no return? What are you, a creature without honor?"

Rabon was about to make a denial, but stopped, suddenly remembering so many things: among them, Dorf's parting words, his curse ringing out over the fields. Wearily he wiped his hand across his mouth and looked into Boran's fiery eyes. "You may be right," he confessed. "I may be without honor. But so is Solmak."

"Honorable or not," he retorted, "he pays his debts. In gold!" And he swung away, beckoning for the crowd to follow.

Caught up by the jostling bodies, Rabon was borne helplessly toward the row of glowing caves. He offered no resistance. Nor did he pretend to a bravery he no longer possessed. What was the use? As he recognized only too well, he was about to join the rest of his small family—Jenna, Dorf, Lal—to share with them the same friendless darkness.

His face pale with dread, lips quivering, he was pitched roughly through one of the cave entrances. Boran was already there, waiting, axe in hand; the expression on his face made it plain that the time for appeals had passed.

At a gesture from Boran, Rabon was again forced to his knees, his head pressed down onto the stone ledge of the pool. From where he lay, he could not see the entrance, but he could hear the shuffle of feet as people crowded into the chamber. He could tell, also, that they were still holding their lanterns because the moving shadows of heads and shoulders crisscrossed the floor all about him. Not until those shadows were still did Boran speak.

"It's well known," he announced in a stern voice, "that of all the gates in this land of ours, the Mountain Gate is the only one that excludes nobody. Provided travelers pay their tribute, they may pass through. That's why we're here now. To exact the required tribute from this boy."

"His head!" someone cried. "Make him pay with his head!"

"So he shall," Boran replied. "That tribute once paid, he too may continue his journey. Though I fancy he'll need a little help from us after this."

One or two people laughed halfheartedly and then fell silent as the shadow of the axe rose. Before it reached the top of its swing, Rabon, his face slick with sweat, clenched his eyes shut. So he did not see how the other shadows suddenly began to stir, to tumble sideways as though felled by some invisible arm; he was ignorant, too, of the vast black shape that took their place, looming across the floor, the walls.

The first he knew of the disturbance was the terrible roar that shattered the silence. Other, fainter cries followed: people shouting in terror, scrambling frantically for the doorway. Still unable to turn, Rabon felt the hands pinning him to the floor slacken their grip; and he rolled clear just as the axe descended, the stone head splintering on the ledge.

He was up instantly, swinging around, his eyes too blurred by steam and sweat for him to see clearly. All he could make out was a hulking shape, like a shadowy spirit of the Lal he had known. He shook his head, blinked, and stared in astonishment at this creature that had come to his aid. As big as Lal, but far more terrifying: its head, its arms, its massive chest, covered in splotches of caked blood; its coarse hair tipped with glistening crystals of frost; a series of livid wounds disfiguring its cheeks and neck. It roared again and reached past him: grasped the struggling figure of Boran and lifted him high.

Rabon had recovered from his fright. Stooping for the shattered remains of the axe, he swung it straight at Boran's defenseless back. But a giant hand jerked out and intercepted the blow.

"No," a voice lisped softly.

And all at once he understood that it was Lal himself who had spoken, not some bodiless spirit; that Lal's eyes were gazing out from the bloodied face; Lal's hands gently wresting the axe from him.

"How . . . ?" he stammered wonderingly.

"Come . . ." Lal interrupted. "Rabon . . . come . . ."

Still holding Boran in one massive fist, Lal ducked through the doorway with Rabon close behind. A flurry of snow struck them in the face, and seconds later several spears thudded into the ground around them.

From one of the lookout posts where the flares still burned, a voice sounded feebly through the windy night. "Release Boran or you both die."

"Kill them anyway!" Boran shouted back, and tried to hit out at Lal, his fists striking uselessly against the arm that held him.

Before any of the guards could obey, Lal chose his own way of dealing with the situation. Picking up one of the long-shafted spears, he hurled it at the gate where it stuck, quivering. "Open . . . !" he roared. Then, to show what would happen if he were ignored, he held Boran high and placed the fingers of one hand around his neck, tightening them just enough for Boran's cry of protest to be choked off.

The message was only too clear, and within seconds small figures were descending the ladders beside the gate; while others came running from the glowing caverns on the far side of the valley.

"No!" Boran screamed, as soon as Lal released the pressure on his throat. "Don't open it! Kill them, I say!"

A few of the figures hesitated, and Lal picked up another of the spears and flung it at the gate with such force that the timber groaned under the impact. A third spear followed, the head striking one of the metal studs embedded in the planking and shattering in a shower of blue-white sparks.

No one held back after that: people hastily released the great locking bar and heaved backward as their leader continued to scream out his disapproval.

Lal, unperturbed by Boran's cries, took something from his belt and pressed it into Rabon's hand. It was the splintered piece of spear Rabon had brought from the swamp. Also tucked into Lal's belt was the knotted club, but he left it there, preferring to rely on their hostage for protection. As the gate swung slowly open, he lumbered forward, still with his hand clasped loosely about Boran's throat. Never once did he glance aside, or even up at the guards peering down from above.

Rabon did, though, and saw the stony glint of weapons pointing down. Closer at hand, he saw something equally daunting: Lal's face momentarily caught in the smoky torchlight. It was crusted with dried blood, one knobbly cheek laid open almost to the bone, the blubbery lips so scarred and cut that the mouth had become a livid gash. Like those watching from above, Rabon could not help drawing away, dropping a pace of two behind as they hurried through the opening.

Once clear of the gate, Lal stopped just long enough to tear from his tunic two thin strips of cloth, which he used to bind Boran's hands and to gag him. That done, he heaved the struggling figure across his shoulder and plodded on.

It was snowing heavily now, the flakes driven with such force by the wind that Rabon felt as if he were under the lash. Then, too, there was the cold, so intense that each breath seemed to sear his lungs. Within minutes his lips were trembling and blue, his hands half frozen to the spear he clutched against his chest. Just above him, sometimes almost obscuring Lal's head and shoulders, the low cloud billowed past, churning back along the valley. While on every side there was nothing but blackness, with only the downward slope to guide them.

Long before midnight, Rabon was stumbling with fatigue — floundering through the occasional drifts of snow or blundering against the tumbled rocks that sometimes littered the valley floor. More than once, his hair plastered flat by an icy covering of snow, he pleaded for a rest. But Lal, perhaps aware that only the act of walking could save them in those conditions, merely quickened his pace, and Rabon, forced to keep up, clutched miserably at the hem of Lal's tunic.

Later still he begged Lal to carry him, and fell into a sobbing, self-pitying rage when the giant again ignored his pleas. "You want me to die, don't you?" he shouted hoarsely, the wind whipping the words from his mouth and carrying them off into the night. "You're jealous of me, that's what you are! Because you're so . . . so . . . !" In his weakened, fuddled state, he could not think what it was that he possessed and Lal lacked. And when he tried to work it out, all he could remember was the way Jenna had gone devotedly to the swamp day after day for her other child. "I hate you!" he shouted, raising his face miserably to the stinging flakes. "I hate you!"

Before the night was half over, even his resentment had left him. Worn out by the freezing temperature and the buffeting of the wind, he needed all his will and strength just to stay alive. No longer fully conscious, he was unaware of how Lal turned back to help him; of how, again and again, he rescued him from the edge of sleep, lifting him gently from the snow and urging him on. Nor did he realize how, in the depths of the night, the giant took refuge beneath a fallen slab of rock and held Rabon's body against his own, rubbing and kneading his chilled limbs until he began to breathe evenly and deeply.

The next thing Rabon knew was that it was morning and he was warm despite the wind, which continued to howl past. He opened his eyes, expecting to glimpse the friendly shape of the sun shining through the cloud, but all he saw was the warty flesh against which he nestled. When he glanced up, there above him was Lal's blood-encrusted face.

Before he could prevent himself, he had started away in disgust — squirming free of Lal's protective arms and crawling to the edge of the rocky hollow in which they were sheltering.

Lal, as always, made no complaint. "Lal . . . ugly . . ." he lisped, nodding his head.

"No," Rabon faltered, suddenly ashamed. "We have to move on, that's all. To where it's warmer!"

Lal nodded again. "Warm . . . good . . ." he agreed. "Eat . . . good . . . too . . ." And he slipped a familiar bundle from his belt. Not the one containing Jenna's remains, which he still guarded jealously, but Rabon's leather rucksack.

The sight of the rucksack served to remind Rabon of his own hunger, and he snatched it from Lal and crammed a handful of grain into his mouth. He was reaching greedily for more when Lal indicated his disapproval.

"Food . . . for man . . ." he murmured, jerking his head to one side.

Rabon had not noticed him until then: Boran, still bound and gagged, watching them from the edge of the hollow, his black hair and frost-pale skin blending easily with the snow-capped boulders among which he lay. He was fully alert, unaffected by the intense cold of the night, his dark eyes glittering with enmity.

Feeling sorry for him, Rabon went over, eased the gag from his mouth, and offered him some of the grain. But he kicked out with both feet, sending it flying in all directions.

"Do you think I'd accept food from Tereu's twin brats?" he said, eyeing them contemptuously. "Look at you both! A hot-headed fool and a monstrosity. No wonder Solmak wants to do away with you. What sane man would acknowledge such sons?"

"You're mistaken," Rabon said coldly. "Solmak fathered only one of us. My mother also knew the spirit of the Night Lord. He's Lal's father."

"Luan!" Boran sneered. "That miserable shadow! No decent woman would accept him as a husband. And even if she did, she'd never survive such a contact."

"She survived," Rabon corrected him. "She lived in the village where I grew up."

"So what would you have me believe?" Boran asked in a jeering voice. "That twins can be sired by two fathers? By the powers of light and darkness? Is that it?"

"Why not?" Rabon replied. "You can see how different we are."

Boran responded with a derisive laugh. "You've heard what they say? How it's a wise man who knows his own child. And a child must be no less wise to know its own father. Or hadn't you considered that?" A sly expression crept over his face. "On the other hand, you may have thought about it just a little too much," he added, addressing only Rabon now. "Maybe you found it less than flattering to call that monster there a full brother, both of you equal progeny of Solmak. Whereas a half-brother . . . and one fathered by the alien spirit of Luan . . . that doesn't sound nearly so bad. It would mean you shared only a mother. And who cares about some unknown slut who . . . ?"

Lal growled and started to his feet, lunging forward, but it was Rabon, far closer, who silenced Boran. Striking out with his clenched fist, he caught him on the side of the head and sent him tumbling backward.

Although his hands were tied, he was up quickly, his face white with hatred. "You thing of dishonor!" he cried, spitting the words out. And he would have run straight at the spear that Rabon had snatched from his belt had Lal not stepped in and heaved them apart.

"No kill!" he roared, tossing Rabon aside. Then to Boran, shaking him until his head lolled drunkenly: "No words . . . bad . . . for mother . . ."

Watching from the soft bed of snow in which he had fallen, Rabon thought at first that Lal was merely angry. Only when he saw the glint of tears in his eyes did he realize his mistake. Wading out of the snow, he went to him, reached up, and touched him gingerly on the hand. "It's all right," he murmured. "What he says doesn't matter. He can't hurt Jenna now."

He wanted to say more, to tell him how, since those dreadful moments in the gully, there was more than a blood-tie between them. But looking up into Lal's face, even more disfigured by the bloody scars of that conflict, he could not bring himself to speak, could not acknowledge openly how much he owed and relied upon this creature from the swamp. He took a deep breath, struggling with himself, with feelings he longed to disown. And while he hesitated, Lal, overcome by his newly awakened grief, shook him off.

"Jenna . . . mother . . . Lal care . . . Lal!" he sobbed—addressing not only Boran, but the world at large: his voice rising steadily, contending with the wind. "Lal care . . . Lal!" he repeated, louder still, as though flinging out a challenge to the craggy peaks.

He had released Boran who lay unnoticed at his feet. His huge body trembling with emotion, he strode some distance down the rocky slope and slumped to his knees. Bent over, his forehead almost touching the ground, he clutched at the sack containing Jenna's remains and hugged it to his chest, nursing it with the same loving care he had given to Rabon during the coldest part of the night. His lips were moving continually, but all that could be heard, borne along by the wind, were snatches of mournful song.

Moved by the sight of his misery, Rabon turned accusingly to Boran. "You!" he cried. "Look what you've done!"

"What *I've* done?" he replied. "Look at yourself before you accuse others, sun-brat."

Rabon tugged him to his feet and shook him. "What do you mean by that?"

"Well, consider your own actions. How you don't just travel with a monster. You treat him as an equal. An equal! This dark worm of life that rises from within our midst once each generation. This grim reminder of what lurks beyond Tereu, in the black heart of the Forbidden City. While others cry out for his destruction, for him to be dealt with as his monstrous nature deserves, you actually side with him against your own kind. Is that normal human behavior? Is it an attitude to inspire trust? I'm not surprised Solmak wants you dead. How could someone like you keep the Sun Gate? You, who of all the sun children since the dawn of time, are the true brother of chaos.

You'd be flinging it open at the first opportunity. Enticing Luan out. Inviting him to cast his evil pall upon the land."

"That's a lie!" Rabon shouted, yearning to lash out once again.

"Go on," Boran taunted him, sensing his intention. "Show me how brave you are. Hit a defenseless man."

"Defenseless?" Rabon replied hotly, rising to the bait. "We'll soon change that!" Thrusting the spearhead between Boran's trussed hands, he began to saw backward and forward—the cutting edge almost slicing through the twist of cloth before he managed to check himself. "Listen," he added more calmly. "We don't need you anymore. You've served your purpose. If I let you go, do I have your word that you'll return to your people?"

"Where else would I go?" Boran answered.

"Then leave us," Rabon said, and jerked the spear upward.

As the cloth binding parted, Boran sprang away—though not back toward the east. Taking three quick strides, he leaped for the cliff that flanked the path they were following: his fingers and toes finding ledges and handholds where there seemed to be none; his agile body working its way rapidly up the smooth surface.

Just before he reached the top there was a roar from Lal, and a huge boulder sailed through the air and smashed into the cliff to Boran's right. A similar warning-shot landed to his left. But fearlessly, amidst a hail of shattered rock, he climbed on, squirming over an outjutting ledge and emerging onto the upper slope.

"You said you'd return to your people!" Rabon shouted indignantly. "You gave me your word!"

"Think back, sun-brat," Boran reminded him and laughed. "I answered you with a question, not a promise."

Incensed by the trick, Rabon picked up a stone and flung it as hard as he could, but it bounced harmlessly off the cliff, far short of its mark. "You cheated me!" he yelled.

"In that case we're even," Boran retorted. "Because you cheated me of the gold I was promised. Well, I may not be able to deliver your head to Solmak, but I can do the next best thing. I can warn him of your coming. Help him prepare a reception for you. That should be worth some reward."

And he ran lightly up the slope, his small figure soon disappearing into a tattered rag of low-flying cloud.

Still feeling cheated, and also a little foolish, Rabon turned to find Lal gazing down at him. His ogre face had never appeared sterner, and he seemed to be clutching Jenna's remains even more protectively, as though he expected those few poor bones to be snatched from him at any moment.

"Bad . . ." he lisped. "People wait . . . for Rabon . . . for Lal . . . bad . . . bad . . ."

Chapter Eleven
Zana

By the following day, the mountains and the intense cold lay behind them. Still a craggy ridge hid from view the hot, low-lying land beyond, but they crossed that shortly before noon and gazed down upon a broad, shallow valley that meandered away into the hazy distance. Once, it may have had a river snaking through it. Now, the lower reaches were the same dull yellow color as the wide slopes on either side. Only where the occasional windmill revealed the presence of a well was there any sign of green—a vivid splash of it, as though an unseen artist had left a casual brushstroke upon the landscape. For the rest, all that grew in the scorching sand were some meager-looking palms, their paper-dry fronds hanging down limply, and a few isolated knots of khaki-colored cactus.

In increasing heat they descended. With their water flask empty, they looked with longing eyes at the nearest of the wells, yet they knew they dare not approach any settlement by day; for if Lal were once sighted, the news would spread like fire along the valley. So they made instead for a grove of palms, which offered cover and a little sparse shade.

It was while they were slogging through the sand toward this grove that Rabon noticed how Lal's footsteps were dragging and how he staggered slightly as he walked.

"Are you all right?" he asked, glancing up at the giant's head, outlined black against the sun.

"Lal . . . tired . . ." he confessed softly.

But the groan he let out as he toppled into the shade spoke of more than tiredness, as did the way his chest heaved and his breath came in quick gasps. For the first time, with a sense of shock, Rabon realized that even Lal's strength had its limits. The desert crossing and the trek through the mountains had been testing enough; on top of that he had taken a terrible beating in the gully, pitting his flesh against the unfeeling rock. Who could say what injuries he had sustained then?

Genuinely concerned, Rabon bent over him, forced himself to look closely at that face he usually avoided. With a pang of guilt, he saw that the wounds, which he had thought of as mere disfigurements, were in serious need of attention. Left untended, still rimmed with dust and dirt from the gully, they had become infected.

"Lal, listen to me," he said. "I'm going to fetch water, and to see if I can get help. Wait here for me."

"Lal . . . come . . . too . . ." he muttered, and tried to rise, only to fall back, his coarse hair matted with sweat.

Creeping to the edge of the grove, Rabon peered out. Quite near at hand, across a field of fresh green, the vanes of a windmill turned idly in the breeze. Beside it was a pool, its surface glittering enticingly. It was too tempting to resist and, bent almost double, he ran to the field and burrowed in among the young plants. Using them as cover, he crawled the rest of the way, emerging at last into the clearing around the pool.

He slaked his own thirst gratefully, thrusting his head and shoulders into the cool, green-fringed margin, wallowing there for some minutes. Refreshed, he took the flask from the rucksack and plunged it far beneath the surface, where the water was coolest.

He was just replacing the stopper when he saw her; a woman approaching the well from the opposite side of the field. Some inner sense warned him that he had already been sighted, but he scurried for cover just the same, flattening himself among the plants.

She came on at an unhurried pace, circled the well, and stopped close to where he lay. Through the green fronds, he could see that she was old, her thick hair completely white, her bare arms and neck grown thin and scrawny. What made him duck back down, however, was her face, which was marked by more than just the years. A blue-colored tattoo ran down her forehead and onto the bridge of her nose—the same tattoo that Jenna had worn, showing twin snakes coiled about a narrow rod.

She was looking not a him, but up at the sky. "There was a time," he heard her say, as though she were addressing the heavens, "when people could walk free in the land of the sun. There was no need for anyone to hide or run away. Especially from an old priestess who carries little violence in her heart."

When Rabon did not move, she looked directly toward him.

"Come, child," she said reprovingly. "Show yourself. You'll receive no hurt from my hand."

Reluctantly, he rose to his feet. But at the sight of him, she staggered back, the earthenware jug she was carrying slipping from her hands.

"Can it be?" she mutterd. "Can it?" She moved hesitantly toward him, stared into the blue depths of his eyes, fingered the fine gold of his hair, ran her hand softly across the olive curve of his cheek. "Your name, child," she asked, "what is it?"

"Rabon."

"Rabon . . ." She seemed to mouth the word, a gleam of anticipation in her eyes. "Ra . . . Ra . . ." she repeated excitedly. "Yes, it's fitting. What she might have chosen." She paused, as if to collect herself for what must come next. "And your . . . your mother . . . is she . . . is she called . . . Jenna?"

Now it was Rabon who was taken aback. "How do you know that?" he gasped.

"Just answer me, boy!"

"Yes, that was her name. She . . ."

"Was?" she took him up sharply. *"Was* her name?"

He lowered his eyes, not just out of respect for Jenna, but to hide his confused feelings from this woman's piercing gaze. "She died of the fever," he murmured. "When the moon was last near the full."

"Dead, you say?" She gave a deep sigh and her lips started to tremble, but with a stern shake of the head she brought her feelings under control. "Near to the full moon," she added wistfully. "Yes, that's fitting too. What she would have wanted. After . . . after . . ."

She broke off and again fixed him with her gray eyes. "There's one other thing I must ask you," she said, a new urgency entering her voice. "And I ask it as a friend. Zana, that's my name. You may have heard your mother speak of me."

He shook his head and saw a shadow of disappointment pass across her face.

"Ah well," she said with a resigned shrug, "perhaps she was trying to forget. Even so, you have to trust me. You see, what I need to know is whether there was a . . . a twin. Another child when you were born. Not golden-haired like you, but . . . different."

"You mean a monster?" he asked bluntly.

Her mouth tightened in angry denial. "No!" she said fiercely. "Not a monster. Different from others, that's all."

There was something about her attitude — an air almost of protectiveness when she spoke of the other child — which decided Rabon.

"Yes, there was a twin," he admitted.

"It survived?" she asked anxiously. "It's alive still?"

"His name is Lal," Rabon told her, "and he's with me here. Except he's sick. I was fetching water for him."

"Water? You need water?" Stooping for her fallen jug, she ran to the pool and filled it. "Where is he?" she asked, straightening up and searching the surrounding landscape. "You must take me to him."

Obediently, he led her across the field to the grove. "There," he said, pointing to where Lal lay moaning softly to himself.

He expected her to back away, horrified by Lal's ugliness. Instead, she knelt over him lovingly. Gathering water in her cupped hand, she poured it tenderly between his scarred lips.

"Drink, my beautiful," she crooned softly. "Drink . . . drink."

Lal's eyelids fluttered open, his eyes settling immediately on her tattoo. "Jenna . . . ?" he murmured. "Mother . . . ?"

"No, not Jenna," she answered. "Only her friend, Zana. But I'll help you if I can."

For the next hour, while the sun plunged toward the horizon, she busied herself washing the caked blood from Lal's face and cleaning his wounds with the fresh well water. By the time she had finished, the late afternoon was deepening into twilight, the blue sky turning a dusky gray. As full night gathered about them, she and Rabon coaxed Lal to his feet and together they made their way slowly through the darkness.

Her house was situated at the outer limits of the valley—a lowly mud dwelling like those in Rabon's home village. At their approach, a guardian snake reared up on the doorsill and had to be eased aside by Zana. Yet even with the doorway free, it was difficult for Lal to enter. Because of his height, he had to crawl through the opening; once inside, his great bulk took up most of the space.

While he lay placidly on the stamped-earth floor, Zana lit a lantern and prepared a porridgy gruel for him to eat—murmuring a lilting song as she spooned the food into his mouth.

Rabon, sitting alone outside, listened to her song with mixed feelings: of envy, of regret, and of loss, too, as though Zana's tender care were something he had almost possessed and then had snatched from him. He could see her through the window space, bending lovingly over the huge mound of Lal's body, and he wondered what it was that drew both Jenna and Zana to this creature of the night; what it was that he himself lacked.

He wondered also about Zana's knowledge of Jenna—a puzzle made all the more intriguing by something he could see hanging in the window space, where it could catch the breeze. It was similar to an object he had glimpsed in the back room of Jenna's house: like a scale, of the kind used for weighing produce, it had a short metal bar; and dangling from either end, two flat metal discs, one as round and yellow as the sun, the other a silver half-moon. Now, in the faint breeze that blew along the valley, the two discs revolved slowly around each other; spinning and flashing in the lantern light, never quite touching;

though in a stronger wind they might easily have clashed and become entangled.

Rabon was watching it curiously when the song ended and Zana brought him a bowl of food.

While he ate, she nodded knowingly toward the revolving shapes. "I can understand your interest in those," she said. "They are a sign, an emblem, for all our people. But as I'm sure you realize, for you and Lal they have a special meaning. Your twin fates, like those discs, are bound to each other. If one of you ceased to exist before the appointed time, the balance would be destroyed."

"What balance?" he asked, laying the empty bowl aside.

"Why, every child within this valley could tell you that," she answered, eyeing him suspiciously. "We are a people under siege, and always have been. As children of the sun, we yet live in fear of the darkness beyond the Sun Gate. No ordinary darkness like this"—she waved her hand airily at the night sky—"but a somber world of madness and chaos, which threatens always to overwhelm us. That's our nightmare, which we live with constantly."

"If it's always there," he responded, "how do we keep it out? Is that what the Sun Gate's for?"

"Partly," she conceded. "Though of itself the Sun Gate would not be strong enough to withstand Luan's power were he roused. Nor is it intended to hold back the vast waters of the ocean. For that there is another gate. The mightiest of all."

"Then how . . . ?"

"Our first line of defense is the tribute. Not just the monthly gift of food, but the greater tribute paid in full by each generation. This is how Luan is appeased, made docile enough for the Sun Gate to contain him. And this also is why Lal is so important to us."

"Important? How?"

"Oh, for most people he's an object of fear. When they look into his face they see only Luan staring out at them. But we of the priesthood know he is more than that. Without his sacrifice we would be lost, the Sun Gate crushed like matchwood. His death will be our protection, a way of satisfying Luan. For it is only by sacrificial death that Luan's destructive nature is appeased. His appetite is such that he craves not just food, but life itself. And were we to deny him, he would reach out and destroy the innocent at will." Her voice had grown sad and, for the second time in the short period he had known her, she shook her head impatiently, refusing to give way to her own deeper feelings. "But of course," she added briskly, "you've heard all this before. Jenna must have explained it to you long ago."

"She explained almost nothing," he confessed.

She gave him another suspicious look. "What about her life in the city of Tereu?" she asked doubtfully. "Her hopes for you? Her fears for Lal? Surely she spoke of such things."

"We . . . we weren't close to each other," he stammered, finding it difficult to make that admission. "I was brought up by someone else. When we did speak, she hardly mentioned her past life."

"So . . ." he heard her murmur thoughtfully, her face invisible in the darkness, "she chose silence as a means of protecting you. Ignorance your only defense in those early years." She nodded her approval. "Yes, and clearly it worked, because you're still alive. Even so, it must have been hard for a young child to bear."

She moved toward him as she spoke and rested her hand lightly on his shoulder, suddenly treating him as tenderly as she had treated Lal. It was what he had hoped for minutes earlier, watching her through the window; yet now, to his surprise, he felt embarrasssed, almost burdened by her touch, and he shrugged her off.

To hide his coldness, he said quickly: "Everyone keeps talking to me in riddles. I understand so little. Can't you explain what's going on? Please?"

He saw her hesitate. "If Jenna chose to keep you in ignorance —" she began.

"But that was far from here," he objected. "I was living in a village beyond the mountains, where no one thought much about the twin cities; where we were cut off by the Mountain Gate and the desert plain. Here it's different. I have a right to know about things now."

Zana turned and stared out into the darkness. A few pinpricks of light, shining from isolated dwellings, showed where the valley wound its way toward the west. "Yes," she admitted reluctantly, "it's different here. Even more different since Solmak took over the guardianship of the Sun Gate."

"So you'll explain?" he asked hopefully.

She did not answer straight away. She went first to the open window, to look in on Lal. Satisifed that he was sleeping peacefully, she came back to where Rabon was sitting and again rested her hand tenderly on his shoulder.

"Where shall I begin?" she asked with a sigh.

Chapter Twelve
Jenna's Story

"Where shall I begin?" Zana asked, sighing as she settled herself comfortably on the sandy ground beside Rabon.

He was silent for a few moments, pondering what to ask first. "Jenna . . ." he said uncertainly, "how did you come to know her?"

"That's easily told," she replied. "There was a time, long ago, when we were sisters in the priesthood. Both of us equals beneath the sun, serving at the monthly ceremonies in Tereu. We shared much together in those days, despite the difference in our ages. Some even mistook us for mother and daughter. But as I say, that was many years ago, before Solmak singled her out."

"Singled her out? For what?"

"She was a beautiful woman," Zana answered simply. "Everyone noticed that, including Solmak. During the ceremonies at the Sun Gate, his eyes would linger on her while the rest of us were watching for Luan's dark shadow. It was as though her beauty alone could banish the fear; that was how he acted anyway, more and more like a man obsessed. So it came as no surprise when he invited her to become his consort."

In spite of himself, Rabon edged closer to the gaunt old woman, taking comfort from her presence. "Did . . . did she accept?" he asked.

Zana gave a bitter laugh. "Solmak has never been the kind of man who worries overmuch about acceptance. He has always taken what he wanted. He is, after all, the ruler of Tereu."

"Yes, but what about her?" he insisted, for suddenly it was important for him to know. "How did she feel about his offer?"

Zana smoothed her robe over her skinny breasts, as though, in recounting what had happened to Jenna, she were also reminded of her own youthful passions. "Oh, she was flattered by his attentions to begin with," she said. "For all I know, she may even have considered accepting him. But that was before she found out what he was really like. Once she knew him better, she responded differently. Not that it did her much good. He had already made a public declaration of his choice of consort, and he wouldn't take no for an answer."

"So what did she do?"

"What can anyone do against someone as powerful as Solmak?" Zana replied wearily. "She tried running away, only to be dragged back by his guards. Next she tried hiding within the city, and met with the same fate—his eyes and ears were everywhere and he soon searched her out. That was when she came to me. 'Help me,' she pleaded desperately, and I could tell from her face that she was prepared to die rather than submit. Which was why I made the suggestion that I did." Zana paused and took a deep breath, like someone preparing herself for a shameful confession. "I told her," she went on, 'If you want to be free of Solmak, there's only one path still open to you.' And I could see straight away that she knew what I meant. Yet I said it just the same, to make sure there was no mistake. Go beyond the Sun Gate, I instructed her, into the Forbidden City. Find Luan. Beg him for protection."

"Luan!" Rabon shuddered and glanced fearfully at the sky, but it was moonless, a black dome softened by scattered starlight. "Why him?" he whispered.

"Who else could she run to?" Zana answered defensively. "He was the only being equal in power to Solmak. A terrible power, but equal. Each of them a supreme ruler within his own city. Luan alone was capable of protecting her, if only to spite Solmak."

"Luan? Protect her?" Rabon said, not trying to hide his disbelief.

"All right," she admitted gruffly, "it was a slim chance. I realized that as well as she did. Still it was the only chance she had."

"How could anyone enter the Forbidden City without Solmak's agreement?" Rabon objected. "As keeper of the Sun Gate, he alone had the power to let people through."

"Ah, so he had," she agreed her manner softening. "But Jenna was a brave and clever woman. She had already seen the golden key that hangs from a chain around Solmak's neck. One night, as he lay sleeping beside her, she eased it out from inside his robe and made an impression of it in soft clay. From that impression was fashioned a second key identical to the first."

"Did she use it?" Rabon asked breathlessly, remembering the way Jenna had once lifted the curtain covering the window of her house and pointed lovingly at the moonlight. "Did she go in search of Luan?"

"Yes, she slipped through the gate one moonless night. Disappeared into that darkness where the waters ebb and flow. For a long time there was no word of her. Then, unexpectedly, she emerged, ready to challenge Solmak with the children she'd carried inside her all along. No ordinary children either. Even then, she somehow knew they were the very twins being looked for by the priesthood."

"Looked for?" Rabon queried. "I don't understand. And how could she challenge Solmak with unborn children?"

Zana studied his face in the faint wash of light from the window. Her own face, old and fringed with a gray bush of hair, was touched now with pity. "Did Jenna not even tell you of our ways as a people?" she asked softly.

"What little I know," he said, "comes mainly from my father . . . I mean the man who brought me up. An old gatekeeper called Dorf."

"A gatekeeper," she repeated eagerly, and gave a murmur of laughter. "So she didn't abandon you. She saw to it that you received some training for what lies ahead."

"What does lie ahead?"

"To understand that, you must first understand the legend of the twins. No, not just a legend," she corrected herself quickly. "A fact. Because in every generation without fail, a special pair of twins appears amongst us. They can be born to anyone: to a member of the priesthood, to one of the people, even to the keeper of the Sun Gate when it happens that she is a woman. Also, the twins can be of either sex."

"Then how do you know if they're the ones?"

"There's never any mistake," she answered confidently. "How could there be, when they're always so different from each other? One always a golden child of the sun, the other a giant figure, a thing of darkness."

"Does that mean Lal and I—?"

She cut him short. "Hear me out. These two children are usually raised by the priesthood—the sun child openly; the giant in secret, though only for his own protection, to stop people from harming him. Were he to walk free, they might mistake him for Luan and stone him to death. Not that death is something he can long avoid, for the fates of the two children are as different as the children themselves. At the appointed time, when they complete their sixteenth year, each takes up the burden of their future. The golden child becomes the new keeper of the Sun Gate. He or she replaces the old keeper who loses all power from that day forward; whose duty it is to don the robe of humility and serve the new keeper. As for the other child, the giant . . ."

She faltered, as though unwilling to go on. But Rabon, preoccupied with what he had already heard, hardly noticed. Springing to his feet, he stared fiercely into the darkness.

"I see," he muttered, as if the night itself were transparent, revealing things his daylight vision could not make out. "What Boran told me is making sense at last. Solmak must have come looking for me, up there in the village, because he knew I'd soon be of age and he'd have to stand aside. So he decided to kill his own son rather than give up his position as Sun Lord."

Zana nodded. "Yes, I saw him pass on his way to and from the mountains, and I guessed then what his purpose was. I thought: history is repeating itself. That gave me heart, because Jenna had outwitted him once, and I believed she would outwit him again."

"Outwit him? How?" He had begun pacing restlessly to and fro, but now he stopped to face her.

"I've already told you how Jenna emerged from the Forbidden City to challenge him," she said slowly. "Well, that was when he first broke with our tradition. Instead of welcoming her and allowing the priest-hood to prepare for the birth of her children, he gave orders that she should be destroyed, orders that would have been carried out if a priest called Pendar had had his way. But again Jenna proved too clever for him. She knew there was no chance of a second escape through the Sun Gate—Solmak now had it heavily guarded. So with some of us to help her, she made it appear that she had scaled the wall. Fresh blood was daubed on the stones, just below the spiked top, to suggest she had been injured while climbing over. I've heard since that it only half convinced Solmak, but still it gave us the time we needed. Time for Jenna and me to flee the city. I came this far with her and would have gone further, but at her insistence she traveled on alone. Dressed as a widow, her tattoo hidden by a mourning band, she made directly for the Mountain Gate while I remained here in exile, awaiting her return."

Rabon had resumed his pacing, and again, toward the end of her account, he was only half listening, unaware of the grief in her voice.

"Solmak!" he said explosively. "He has more to answer for than I thought. There's not just Dorf. Nor just what he did to me. There's Jenna too. Well, we'll see who's going to die. We'll see." And drawing the spearhead from his belt, he flourished it recklessly.

Zana had also risen, her face a cold mask of disapproval. "What?" she said sternly. "You'd do violence to your own father?"

"Why not?" he flashed back.

"Because then you'll be as bad as Solmak. Your duty is to reason with him, not kill him."

"I've tried that and—"

"Then try it again," she broke in.

"You mean put myself in his power?" His voice rose in disbelief.

"Yes, that's exactly what I mean. Don't forget we rescued Jenna. If we have to, we can rescue you as well. Arrangements have been made for just that possibility."

"And leave him unpunished?" he nearly shouted.

"It's not for us to punish him!" she shouted back. "The people will do that for us. When Luan remains unappeased—when his appetite for death drives him to release the great waters of the ocean to plunder the city of Tereu—they'll soon send Solmak packing. They won't stand by and watch their loved ones being taken, their farmland ruined. The fertile land is precious. Without fertile produce, Tereu's markets would be useless. Tereu itself would become almost as deserted as the Forbidden City. Only the priesthood would be left."

"Well, you can rely on the people if you want to," he countered passionately, "but I've tried that too. And it didn't help me or Dorf. That's why I'm relying on myself from now on."

"Where are you going?" she called sharply, because he had tucked the spear back into his belt and was already marching off into the night.

"To find Solmak," he called back. "To do what should have been done nearly fifteen years ago."

"What? You? A boy? Against Solmak and his guards?"

For all his anger, he was tempted to stop. "Someone has to do something about him," he grated out, ploughing doggedly on across the sandy slope.

"And Lal?" she cried desperately, as he disappeared into the darkness. "What about him?"

She heard his footsteps stop. His voice floated toward her, oddly plaintive. "You said our paths lie in different directions."

"Yes, but not yet. Until the end of your sixteenth year your fates are bound to each other."

The footsteps—dragging, reluctant—were heard again, and he appeared at the outer edges of the lamplight. "You never said what happens to him when . . . when the time comes," he said, speaking more calmly now.

"Do you care?" she challenged him.

He shrugged, lingering there where the shadow and the light met. "Just tell me," he said.

She dropped her gaze, rubbed a gnarled hand across her forehead. "I spoke earlier of how Luan must be appeased if his appetite for death is to be kept under control. So once every generation, when the giant twin enters his seventeenth year, the Sun Gate is lifted and he is . . . is fed to Luan."

"Fed?" he echoed her, hardly able to believe what he had heard. "Did you say fed?"

She nodded sadly. "The old legends tell us he devours the child. That is how his hunger is assuaged."

"No!" he protested, running back toward her. "I won't let it happen!"

"You speak like Solmak," she reproved him. "He also wants to destroy our traditions."

"But it's so . . . so cruel."

"It would be crueler still to rouse Luan." She swung around and pointed to the ritual discs hanging in the window. "If the balance is destroyed, if Luan were simply to unleash the might of the ocean upon us, then . . . then . . ."

"Then?"

"It will be you the people will turn on. You and Lal together who will be fed to him."

"Is there no other way?"

"None."

That one word, so final, sounded in his ears like the thud of the village gate closing at nightfall. And yet—it came back to him unex-pectedly—Dorf had once reopened the gate, many years before, so Jenna could enter.

"I don't care what you say," he added stubbornly. "I won't let Sol-mak do that to him."

"Solmak?" she asked, surprised—and taking him by the shoulders, she held him at arm's length. "Tell me, Rabon," she said softly, "do you love Lal?"

Love? He was caught off guard by the question. Hastily, he recalled all the things Lal had done for him, the many times he had saved his life. There was so much to repay. So much to be grateful for. But love . . . ? For that face! That lumbering body!

"No, not love," he answered truthfully.

She nodded, as though in relief. "That's just as well," she said. "Because it isn't for Solmak to push Lal through the Sun Gate. That's always the first duty of the new Sun Lord."

It took a few seconds for her meaning to sink in. Then, with a hurt cry, Rabon pulled free and stumbled over to the window. Lal was sprawled just inside the opening, fast asleep, his huge chest rising and falling. Mercifully his face was turned away. Seeing him lying there, so peaceful and defenseless, Rabon was taken with a sudden wild idea—of leading him back across the mountains, of hiding him in the swamp once again, the two of them spending the rest of their lives there. Yes, he thought excitedly, yes! He pictured to himself their imaginary life together, almost believing in it until his eyes lighted on the sack hanging from Lal's belt; the sack containing Jenna's remains, which was his reason for being here now.

Straight away Rabon's dream collapsed. There was no escape. Asking Lal to turn back would be like asking him to abandon Jenna. It was unthinkable. He had vowed to bury her where she belonged, and he would keep to it. Much as he, Rabon, had made a vow to Dorf: to avenge his cruel death—a promise no less binding than Lal's. No, for neither of them was there any going back. Come what may, they had to pursue their journey to its end.

Behind him, Zana murmured: "It's as I told you. For the present, your fates are bound together. All of us it seems, me included, must share a single road."

Rabon made no reply. The night, previously so warm and close, felt abruptly chill. The breeze from along the valley made him shiver. It also stirred into motion the twin discs hanging directly above his head, causing them to circle uneasily around each other.

Chapter Thirteen
Twin Cities

Lal's natural strength enabled him to recover quickly, and after a few days they set out for the city of Tereu. Traveling only by night, keeping always to the wasteland that bordered the winding valley, they easily escaped detection by any of Solmak's spies; and on the morning of the third day they neared their destination. As dawn broke over the stony wilderness through which they were trudging, they caught their first glimpse of the sea.

Rabon, who had heard only vague descriptions of it, was too astonished to move, having never dreamed that so much water existed in the world. Lal, on the other hand, gave a crow of delighted laughter and immediately began scrambling down to where the foam-topped waves crashed against the shore.

"Stop!" Zana called out sharply, making him lumber to a halt. "Those are dangerous waters, filled with sharp-toothed creatures that can match even your strength."

"Drink . . ." he explained, pointing to their nearly empty waterbags.

She shook her head and drew him gently back up the slope.

"It's not like well water," she explained patiently. "You'll go mad if you drink that."

"Mad?" Rabon queried, still gazing in wonder at the vast expanse of glittering blue. "But why? It's so . . . so beautiful."

"Don't be misled by the loveliness of it, boy," she cautioned him. "What you see before you is not what it seems. All this water" — she swept her arm out toward the horizon — "is so heavy with salt that it's useless. If it once floods any portion of farmland, nothing will grow there for years. Luan's curse, that's what we call it."

At the mention of Luan, Rabon turned hastily away. That name, like the name of Solmak, cast a cloud over the brightening morning, reminding him once again of what awaited him: a contest he could neither avoid nor yet hope to win. For even if he defeated Solmak and avenged Dorf's needless murder, what then? He in turn would be called on to commit murder, to sacrifice Lal to the dark shadow lurking beyond the Sun Gate. He shrank from the prospect. It seemed almost preferable to submit to Solmak, to give *himself* up to death. Except that he could not do that either, not with the memory of Dorf's death still so fresh in his mind.

Trapped and unhappy, he followed Zana and Lal, who were already making their way along the rocky coastline, the waves constantly pounding away at the shore below.

After an hour of walking through the mounting heat, they reached a point where they could gaze down upon the valley. It had broadened considerably, a dish of fertile land dotted with hundreds of windmills and pools and bright green fields. And there, snuggled within the lush growth, was the city of Tereu.

Rabon, who had been half-expecting a larger version of his village, was again taken by surprise. Here there were no mud huts set in an open space, but row upon orderly row of stone-built houses, many of them several stories high. Tiny gardens flourished behind each dwelling, and even some of the roofs were planted with grass and bushes. Between the rows of houses, there were long thoroughfares, all as straight and orderly as the houses themselves, with streams of people and wagons moving along them.

There was one other feature of the city that, to Rabon, was equally unexpected. On its eastern margin it had no protection; the streets led directly into the surrounding farmland. Only on its western boundary was there a wall. Made of stone, and almost as deep as it was high, it ran right across the valley and slotted into sheer cliffs on either side. Far taller than any of the houses, it was crowned along its entire length by metal spikes designed to impale anyone trying to cross it. Beyond those spikes, on the westward side of the wall, lay what was obviously the Forbidden City.

A sharper contrast could hardly have been imagined. Unlike Tereu, it was not laid out in neat squares; nor were its buildings set in green surrounds. Only shadow reigned there—most of its houses dank and crumbling away, their salt-encrusted walls cracked and corroded by long exposure to the sea wind. Its many thoroughfares—for it occupied a vast area—were not only deserted, but awash, so they looked like dark rivers. These rivers curved and looped in every possible direction, crisscrossing and intertwining to form a patternless maze that led nowhere but back into itself.

The only thing that this far bigger city had in common with Tereu was that it, too, was flanked on its western margin by a wall. Though this wall, even seen from a considerable distance, was obviously much higher and thicker. Like the outer rampart of some stone fortress, it jutted boldly into the sea, holding the waters at bay.

"There lies the secret of Luan's power," Zana declared, pointing toward the distant wall. "If the whim took him, he could open the Moon Gate and flood the valley with salt water."

"And the Sun Gate?" Rabon asked.

Now she pointed to the smaller of the two walls, the one separating the cities. "That's where you'll find the Sun Gate. As I explained before, it's not designed to hold back the dark waters. It's there for the same reason as that long row of spikes; to keep Luan from entering the city."

"So is that the real task of the Sun Lord?" Rabon asked. "To protect us from Luan?"

She nodded. "It's a task that involves more than keeping the gate. As well as enforcing all our laws, the Sun Lord also has to see that the monthly tribute is paid. Without that, Luan becomes restive. Uncontrollable. Then, too, there's the question of . . . of sacrifice . . ."

She broke off and glanced knowingly toward Lal. But unaware that

he was being discussed, he had unknotted the sack from his belt.
"Home . . ." he lisped softly, as though addressing the grisly remains
within the sack, ". . . home . . . for mother . . ."

"Yes," Zana agreed, patting him affectionately, "this is where she
was born. If you look over there, toward that row of houses . . ."

Again she was forced to break off, for it was clear that Lal was
gazing in an entirely different direction, his eyes fixed longingly on
the watery maze of the Forbidden City.

"No, not there," she corrected him. "I mean here, in Tereu."

He shook his head, clutching the sack now as if he feared Zana
might snatch it from him. "Mother say . . . city . . . near water . . ." he
murmured.

"I tell you she was born in Tereu. No one lives in the Forbidden
City. It was given over to Luan and the tidal waters long ago. In a
past too distant for anyone to remember."

"Tereu . . . not home . . ." he insisted. "Jenna say . . . other one . . .
home . . ."

Zana turned to Rabon. "He trusts you," she said. "Explain to him
that he can't take her remains into the Forbidden City. He'd be destroyed."

But Rabon, his eyes downcast, refused to answer.

"Explain it to him!" she almost shouted.

He looked up grudgingly, his young face closed against her. "He
has to go in there sometime," he muttered. "Why not now?"

"Because his time hasn't come yet," she snapped. "There's more
than a year of life left to him. You can't rob him of that. He has so
little already."

When Rabon again remained silent, she grabbed the front of his
tunic and shook him angrily. "Come to your senses, boy!" she hissed.
"You can't avoid your responsibilities like this. You'll only add regret
to the guilt you're already feeling."

"How do you know what I'm feeling?" he answered sullenly.

"All right," she conceded, "maybe I don't. But I do know what your
duties are. They're not just to sacrifice him to Luan when the time
comes. You have to protect him until that time. Much as he's protected
you."

He tossed his head in distress. "How can I —?" he began.

"Have you forgotten that he's your brother?" she interrupted. "That he's the other half of yourself?" And she would have shaken him again if Lal had not intervened.

"No fight . . ." he said, gently parting them. "Fight . . . bad . . ."

"Yes, bad," she echoed him bitterly, "but not half as bad as your brother here. A Sun Lord in the making, that's what he is. With eyes as hard as Solmak's, and a heart to match!"

It was Lal who contradicted her. "Not bad . . ." he said, smiling at Rabon. "Good . . . good . . ."

"D'you hear that?" she declared. "He still believes in you, even though you're prepared to let him go to his death."

Rabon looked around unhappily, as though expecting Lal to rescue him yet again. Which in a sense is what happened, for the giant nodded reassuringly at him.

"No . . . stop . . . Lal . . ." he said firmly. "Lal . . . take Jenna . . . other city . . . tonight . . ."

At that point something inside Rabon very nearly rebelled. Yet, although his young face twitched uncontrollably, no sound came from his lips.

"Solmak's true son!" Zana spat the words at him.

"It's Lal's choice," he answered desperately. "Not mine."

"You'll be the one who'll have to open the gate for him. Do you realize that?"

"But I don't have a key," he protested.

"You can't wriggle out that easily, my boy," she answered in a mocking voice, patting the space between her withered breasts. "You remember my telling you about the key Jenna used to enter the Forbidden City? Well, I have it here. If we manage to reach the Sun Gate tonight, it's yours. To do with as you will. What do you say to that?"

But once again he had nothing to say. All he could do was stare miserably before him — at the city of Tereu, so deceptively beautiful in the sunlight.

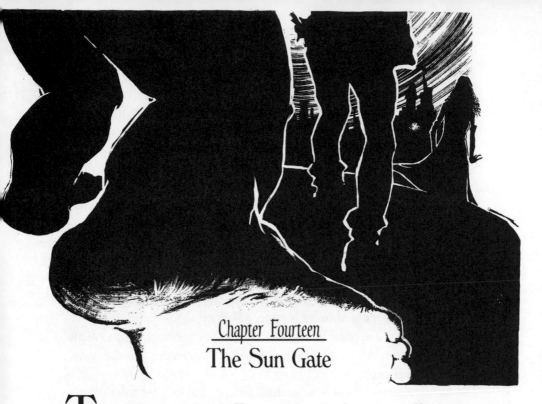

Chapter Fourteen
The Sun Gate

They did not approach Tereu until well after sunset. For some hours they watched the lights of the city winking out, and only when most of the houses were in darkness did they descend the side of the valley.

Cautiously they entered the first long street and peered around them. There was no one in sight; the houses were closed and silent, the waxing moon hidden by a bank of cloud. Somewhere in the distance they could hear the tramp of heavy footsteps, like soldiers marching in step, and after that, nothing but a whirr of insect noise in the humid atmosphere of the night.

Encouraged, they hurried on, skirting the open marketplaces, keeping always to the narrowest streets where they were least likely to be spotted. Occasionally, spying some lonely figure returning home late, they huddled together in a doorway until the danger was past. And once, surprised by a sudden flash of lantern light, they scurried into the nearest garden and crouched in a cluster of bushes. But neither then nor later were they challenged, and soon they were padding along in the shadow of the wall, heading directly for the Sun Gate.

Shortly before reaching it, they again heard heavy footsteps and quickly withdrew into the darkened space beneath a stone archway.

The footsteps grew louder, flares appeared at the end of the street, and an armed guard came marching toward them. In the flickering torchlight, Rabon could see two lines of soldiers—one armed with spears, the other carrying woven baskets. Among the soldiers were three other figures whom he recognized instantly. The tall gray-haired priest called Pendar, a shield strapped to his right arm; Boran jogging along behind him, his dark eyes darting suspiciously from side to side; and in the very center of the column, guarded against any possible attack, the unmistakable figure of Solmak. At each step the torchlight flashed on his golden helmet, on his glittering body armor, on his snake-entwined staff; while from the upper part of his left arm there were jewel-like glints as the live viper slowly turned its head toward the darkness.

The sight of Solmak striding so arrogantly through the night reawakened all Rabon's former hatred. "Curse him!" he grated out, clutching the spearhead and moving forward menacingly.

"Don't be hasty, child!" Zana whispered, tugging at the hem of his tunic. "Now's not the time for a challenge. Not when he's so heavily guarded."

He hesitated, and in those few moments of delay the column passed them by. Soon, all they could hear were receding footsteps, which stopped abruptly and were followed by loud clanging.

"What's that?" Rabon asked, emerging from the archway.

Zana was shaking her head, as if in regret. "I should have realized," she muttered to herself. Then, to Rabon: "I fear we're on a fool's errand. This, out of all nights in the month, is no time to approach the Sun Gate." Even as she spoke, the darkness paled slightly, and a perfect half-moon slid out from behind the bank of cloud. "See," she said, looking upward, "it's the night of the first quarter. When Luan comes to the Sun Gate to collect his tribute. That's where Solmak is now. It's no place for us. Not with the Sun and Night Lords both present."

She turned, ready to move back along the street, but neither Lal nor Rabon attempted to follow.

"Lal go . . . Sun Gate . . . now . . ." he said, placing one hand on the sack at his waist.

"But it's a bad time for you to enter the Forbidden City," she replied. "Didn't you hear what I said? Luan always comes for his tribute when the moon reaches its first quarter. That's what the clanging's for—to summon him."

"Lal . . . no wait . . ." he said doggedly. "Mother . . . rest . . . soon . . ."

"What difference can one more night make?" she responded irritably. "She's already waited long—"

"No," Rabon cut in, "Lal's right. If he has to meet Luan, tonight's as good a time as any. It's the same for me. What's the use of running away from Solmak? I have to challenge him sooner or later."

"Then let it be later," she said quickly. "For both of you. Because I tell you truly, if you go to the Sun Gate tonight, there's a good chance you'll both die."

Her voice had dropped to a whisper, her face so grave that Rabon almost wavered. Only Lal refused to be swayed.

"Tonight . . . for Jenna . . ." he said, speaking solemnly, "not for . . . Lal . . ."

Not for Lal! The truth of those simple words struck home to Rabon. "Yes," he affirmed with sudden resolution. "We're here for the sake of Jenna and Dorf. Not for ourselves." And leaving Zana standing in the empty street, he followed Lal.

The clanging stopped just as they reached the top of a flight of stone steps. By then, and much against her will, Zana had rejoined them.

"Luan will soon be approaching," she advised Rabon in a whisper. "If you're to challenge Solmak, do it while Luan's there to distract him."

With Lal towering above him, Rabon crept to the bottom of the steps and peered around the corner. Before him lay a torchlit courtyard, exposed to the skies, but bounded at its farther end by the wall. At the top of the wall, he could just make out a dark pattern of spikes, and at its base, an even darker opening. That opening was not fitted with a heavy wooden door, as he had imagined, but with a woven metal grille through which he could spy a glitter of swirling water. Hardly more than a latticed shutter, it offered no barrier to the dark waters beyond, nor did it appear stout enough to withstand even a chance encounter with the fabled strength of the Night Lord. Then, as one of the torches sputtered and flared, he saw, through the gaps in the grille, that its whole outer face was studded with deadly rows of spikes — all of them pointing toward the Forbidden City to prevent Luan approaching too close.

"The Sun Gate," he breathed out, and heard Zana's grunt of assent from behind.

He now saw that the lower part of the gate was awash with murky water that spilled in through the open mesh and formed shallow puddles on the courtyard floor. Many of the guards were now splashing through these puddles, carrying their heavy baskets, laden with food, to a much smaller grille set into the wall beside the gate. It was Solmak who opened it for them, standing to one side as they pushed the baskets through the opening.

"The tribute," Zana murmured softly.

Rabon nodded, his eyes fixed on Solmak who was partly obscured by the procession of guards. As the last basket disappeared, however, Solmak turned to close and lock the grille, and for the first time his back was left unprotected, the soft, unarmored flesh of his neck clearly visible.

It was the chance Rabon had been looking for, yet for a split second he held back. Wasn't this man his natural father? How then could he kill him? How? The answer, as always, came in the form of a remembered image — of Dorf's kindly face smiling at him. And casting all other considerations aside, he groped for the spearhead, his arm already drawing back when Zana clutched at his wrist.

"No!" she pleaded in a fierce whisper. "You're here to challenge him. Not kill him. Not your own father!"

She was still struggling with him when, from beyond the wall, there came heavy splashing. All at once a shadow loomed across the gate. Such a shadow as Rabon had never dreamed of. So huge and forbidding that he, like everyone else, could not take his eyes from it.

"Now," Zana was insisting, "go to Solmak, plead with him. While you have the chance."

With an effort, Rabon shifted his attention from the gate and pushed Zana aside. Only to be distracted yet again, by a snuffling sound from close beside him. He glanced around and saw that Lal was straining forward, his eyes wide and staring, muffled cries breaking from his lips.

"Keep quiet!" Zana muttered urgently.

But already the noise had given away their presence. Boran, ever watchful, had whirled around.

"They're here!" he cried. "Look out!"

There was a period of mild confusion—with Zana clinging onto Lal, trying to restrain him, and some of the guards running this way and that. And quickly, before he could change his mind, Rabon moved out into the open and flung the spearhead.

It was a hasty throw, but still would have found its mark had it not been for Pendar. Stepping foward, he thrust the shield out just in time: the spearhead, instead of striking Solmak's chest, glanced off the shield's metal edge and shot through a gap in the woven grille of the Sun Gate, straight toward Luan's shadow.

There was a kind of thud, and from the darkness came a groan of pain and surprise, so loud it stilled every other sound. Momentarily, no one moved, the faces of the guards strained and haggard in the torchlight. Then, with a choking cry, Lal tore himself free of Zana and charged straight at the Sun Gate, scattering the guards before him.

He hit it with such force that it bulged outward, the metal joints shrieking in protest. When it failed to give way, he began beating at it. The whole structure shuddered under this fresh assault, flakes of stone breaking from around the bolts that fastened it to the wall.

"Stop him!" Solmak yelled. "If he smashes the gate . . . !"

A few of the guards rallied, as did Boran and Pendar who had snatched spears from the men nearest to them. In a half circle, they closed in, while Lal continued to hammer away. He stopped as some of the spears prodded nervously at him. Turning, he gave one of his great roars, sending his attackers tumbling backward. But as he resumed his hammering they regrouped and advanced now in a more determined line.

'We have to help him!" Zana cried, and sprang forward. But she was struck down by the first guard she encountered, the man felling her with the weighted end of his spear.

That spurred Rabon into action. The next moment, he too was running across the courtyard, dodging beneath a swinging spear, leaping at the line of guards that hedged Lal in.

It was a quick, pointless struggle, his young strength no match for theirs. Within seconds Boran had wrestled him to the ground and Pendar's heavy shield pinned him there; the dagger end of Solmak's staff pressed into his throat.

"Look, monster!" Solmak called loudly. "Watch how your brother dies!"

The hammering at the Sun Gate ceased abruptly and Lal swung around. He took one lumbering step . . . and stopped as Solmak made as if to bear down on the staff.

"It's in your power to save him, Moon Whelp," Solmak added. "Give yourself up and he lives. You both live."

Lal seemed to sway slightly, like a giant tree blown by a stormy wind. Moving his head ponderously from side to side, he looked first at Rabon, lying helpless before him, and then at the gate. Still staring at the gate, he clutched at his pendulous ears with both hands, as if in despair. Deep in his throat there sounded an agonized cry. It was directed not at Solmak, but at the shadow beyond the wall. From the darkness there came an answering cry, deeper still, followed by loud splashing. Gradually the splashing grew fainter, until at last the water at the foot of the gate lay placid and still once more.

There were tears of regret in Lal's eyes, and of longing, too, as he faced his tormentors. With a shudder he dropped to his knees, let his head droop forward in an attitude of submission. Yet his voice was firm, decided. "Lal . . . no fight . . . Solmak . . . no kill . . ."

Chapter Fifteen
The Pit

It was like being back in the barren lands: the sun, searingly hot, beating down into the pit where they had been thrown. For Zana it was worst of all. Old, with her head still throbbing from the blow she had received, she lay on the rough floor panting in distress and although Lal crouched over her, shielding her from the sun's direct rays, the heat reflecting off the rock walls made her moan softly.

Once, at the hottest part of the day, Solmak and Boran came to observe them. With Pendar hovering silently in the background, they stood on the rim of the pit gazing mockingly down.

"What are you going to do with us?" Rabon asked, his voice hoarse from thirst.

"Do?" Solmak said in surprise. "But it's already done. You've been given to the sun. As are all those who come here seeking darkness. That's the law."

"It wasn't darkness I was looking for," Rabon called back. "It was my father. My *natural* father."

He meant it as an accusation, certain that Solmak would show some reaction, but the Sun Lord merely smiled. "Is that the usual way for a child to greet its father?" he asked. "With a sharpened spearhead?"

Before Rabon could reply, he and his companions had moved away, leaving the rim of the pit empty except for the persistent dazzle of sunlight.

"So he's going to let us die," Rabon muttered, slumping down in despair. "To let the sun wither us up. And there's nothing we can do about it!"

"No . . . something . . . to do . . ." Lal responded, nodding his head encouragingly.

Rabon looked up. "You mean you can get us out of here?"

"Lal . . . throw . . . Rabon . . ." he lisped, pointing to the top edge of the pit.

"As high as that?" Rabon asked, squinting up through the glare.

"Arms . . . strong . . ."

"But then how would *you* get out?"

"Lal . . . stay . . . Rabon . . . go . . ."

Despite the heat, Zana had rolled onto her side and was watching them intently. Conscious of her eyes upon him, Rabon turned toward her.

"You expect me to leave him here, don't you?" he said half guiltily.

She gave a weary sigh and sank back. "There's no need for either of you to be left behind," she assured him. "If you're patient, you can both get out."

"I don't see how," he answered, staring glumly at the smooth walls of the pit.

"Pendar doesn't speak for the whole priesthood," she said shortly. "There are still some of us who remain true to our traditions."

For the time she would say no more than that, and it was not for some hours that the meaning of her words became clear.

The sun had set, bringing some relief to the captives. As the first stars began to appear, there was a rustle of footsteps and a knotted rope snaked down into the pit. It had barely touched bottom when the golden-haired figure of a young priestess came quickly down.

A smile of silent understanding passed between her and Zana.

"So you remembered my warning," Zana said.

"I swore a vow," she answered, bowing to the old woman.

"And you'll honor that vow? You'll give up your own life if necessary?"

She did not hesitate. "I will."

"Good," Zana muttered. Then, her arm around her companion, she turned toward Lal and Rabon. "This is Nari," she explained. "We come from the same part of the valley and I've known her since she was a baby. She's here to help you escape. So listen carefully. First—"

"We have a rope," Rabon cut in. "What are we waiting for?"

"If you'll curb your impatience for once," she said sternly, "you'll find out. First of all, you, Rabon, must take this key so that you can open the Sun Gate." And she drew a golden key from beneath her robe and handed it to him. "Next, you'll have to exchange clothes with Nari."

"Exchange clothes?" he queried. "But . . ."

"Just listen to me," she insisted. "There's no time for argument. Now, the key. Take it straight to the Sun Gate. Unlock and raise the gate so it looks as though Lal has escaped into the Forbidden City. When Solmak finds it open, he'll abandon the search. Meanwhile you must both make for the barren lands. At this time of night, you should be able to get out of Tereu unnoticed. Once you're clear, keep going. Get as far away as you can."

"What about you?" he asked.

"I'm staying here with Nari. She's about your size and coloring. She should be able to pass for you, especially in your clothes. Anyone gazing down from above will assume that Lal's the only one missing. They'll think he used his great strength to get out. It could be days before Solmak discovers the truth. By then you'll be well away."

It was a tempting plan, Rabon had to admit that. But as always there was Dorf's memory to be considered—Rabon's desire for vengeance his one and only reason for coming to Tereu. Also, there was the way Zana had looked at him earlier that day, when Lal had offered to let him escape alone: her lined face already clouded with bitter knowledge of him.

"No," he said, trying to appear braver than he felt, "we can't leave anyone here. Either we all escape or we all stay."

Lal was nodding his head. "All . . . all . . ." he affirmed.

Unexpectedly, Zana smiled at Rabon—for the first time in days it seemed. "That's all very well," she answered gently, "but how far do you think we'll get? With nothing to delay him, Solmak will run us down in no time."

"He didn't run you and Jenna down."

"That was different. He half believed Jenna had returned to the Forbidden City."

The Forbidden City! The answer to their problem occurred to Rabon in a flash, much as it had once occurred to Zana years before.

"There is . . . another way," he stammered. "One we could . . . that Solmak wouldn't . . ."

"Out with it, child."

He made himself speak before he lost his nerve. "The Sun Gate. We could escape through there."

Even Nari, so calm until then, started back. "Are you mad?" she asked. "Luan or one of his creatures would soon do Solmak's work for him. You wouldn't live to see the sunrise."

"Jenna lived," he said softly. "And Zana here was the one who gave her the idea."

"But even if you survived, you'd never get out again. It's an endless maze. You'd be lost forever."

He returned her steady gaze. "My mother wasn't lost. She emerged unharmed months later."

"She was lucky," Zana began. "She—"

"No, not lucky," Rabon interrupted. "Luan spared her. And there's Lal here to prove that's true. Where else would he get his face and size but from Luan?"

"Do you understand what you're saying?" Zana almost shouted. "That Jenna lay with Luan as well as with Solmak! That her twin children were engendered by two different . . ."

But Nari, alarmed by the noise they were making, held a warning finger to her lips. "Quiet!" she whispered. "Or no one will get out of this pit alive."

"You're right," Rabon agreed. "There's been more than enough talk. Let's decide. Do we hide in the Forbidden City, or do we stay?"

"Whatever else you are," Zana grumbled, already hobbling over to the rope, "you're Jenna's son. I'll grant you that. Just as stubborn as she ever was."

With Lal to help her, and with a great deal of groaning and complaining, she managed to climb from the pit. The others soon joined her at the top—Lal pulling the rope back up and coiling it around his waist.

They were standing in an open space bounded by a circular mud-brick wall. There was only one gap in the wall, which normally would have been guarded, but now the guard lay sprawled in the moonlight, his eyes closed, the shattered remains of a bottle on the ground beside him.

"Don't worry," Nari assured them, pointing to the dark stain that had spilled from the broken bottle, "he should sleep soundly until morning."

Stepping over his body, they emerged into a quiet part of the city. Between two buildings they could see a fountain, its jet flashing silver in the moonlight; gratefully they ran over to drink and fill the leather bags Nari had brought with her. That done, they set off through the silent streets.

The route Nari chose enabled them to keep mainly to the shadows. Yet despite all their caution, there were times when they had no choice but to venture out into the open. It was on one of these occasions that they were spotted. A warning cry rang out, and all at once their steady progress through the city became a desperate flight.

Figures appeared at almost every corner now; armed groups clattered after them until Lal turned and frightened them off. But still the warning cries sounded on every side—with doors opening, lanterns swinging out into the night, fearful faces searching the shadows. Soon Zana, unable to stand the pace, was being carried by Lal, and they were ducking and weaving in a frantic attempt to stay ahead of their pursuers.

"Down there!" Nari gasped, and pointed to a flight of stone steps that Rabon instantly recognized.

Thankfully, believing they were safe at last, they descended to the courtyard fronting the Sun Gate. But already they were too late. Three guards, led by Boran, were waiting there for them.

"You've escaped once too often, Sun Brat," he sneered, glaring at Rabon. "There's no way forward from here, not with the Sun Gate locked. And if you look behind you, you'll find there's no way back."

There was a bustle of activity at the top of the steps and more guards blocked their retreat.

"Stand aside, Boran," Rabon warned him, his voice shrill and desperate. "This isn't your gate to keep."

"Nor is it yours. Not yet. Not ever, if Solmak has his way. And he will, I promise you that. Especially now that Luan is no longer the threat he was."

"Not a threat? What are you talking about?"

Boran laughed and half lowered the axe he was holding. "As if you didn't know already," he chuckled. "You, the one who threw the spear; who heard it hit its mark out there in the darkness."

There was a growl from Lal, but Boran was laughing again. "A clean hit it must have been," he went on. "Judging by the groan he let out anyway. Who's to say what damage you might have done? Why, with luck, Tereu may be rid of his dark presence forever. The Sun Lord will be the sole ruler here, while Luan lies dead somewhere . . ."

He was not given the chance to finish. Letting out a mournful howl, Lal lumbered forward, the knotted rope whirling in his hands. The end of it caught Boran around the thighs and sent him crashing back into the other guards, all four of them tumbling together across the courtyard.

"Quick! The key!" Zana called, darting toward the Sun Gate.

Rabon and Nari were close behind her; while Lal, still howling mournfully, still whirling the rope, defended their rear.

His hand trembling under the stress of the moment, Rabon slipped the golden key into the lock and turned it. There was a click as a line of bolts snapped back: suddenly the metal grille was no longer attached to the sides and base of the opening.

"Pull!" Nari instructed him, and he reached down into the swirling water and tugged as hard as he could—the gate creaking and groaning as it slid upward.

Behind them there were cries of dismay, the word *Luan* being shouted hysterically. Turning, they saw that the guards were retreating, shoving at each other in their eagerness to get away; those in the rear casting terrified glances behind them. Within seconds the courtyard was almost clear. Only one of them remained: Boran. He had retrieved his axe and was creeping up behind Lal.

"Lal!" Nari and Rabon yelled together.

The giant, still intent upon the retreating guards, turned slowly, momentarily defenseless, open to the axe, which was about to descend. But for Zana, it would have bitten into him. She stooped for a fallen spear and hurled it straight at Boran. At such close range, it did not matter that the throw was clumsy and inexpert. The sharpened head did its work just the same: it struck Boran between the shoulder-blades and passed through into his chest.

He must have died instantly for the axe rumbled from his hands and his body toppled forward into Lal's waiting arms.

The giant lowered him gently to the ground. Easing the spear from the body, he flung it away. Then, gentle again, he wiped the blood from the slack mouth.

"Come on, Lal," Rabon urged him, for already they could hear the noise of people approaching. Not this time the ordinary soldiers of the city, but Solmak's personal guard. There was a flash of gold, and Pendar himself edged down the steps, his gaunt body hidden by a protective shield.

Giving Boran a last pat, Lal joined Rabon and Nari at the opening. But as Zana made as if to accompany them, he stopped her.

"No . . . come . . ." he lisped softly. "Tereu . . . for Zana . . . only . . . Tereu . . ."

"Don't be a fool!" Rabon broke in. "She has to come with us."

"Lal . . . say . . . no . . ." he replied firmly.

"But Lal . . ." Nari began.

Zana silenced her with a wave of the hand. "I know what he's saying" she said. "And maybe he's right. After what I've just done, maybe I do belong here. Like it or not, I've become one of Solmak's people."

There was no more time for argument. A spear sailed across the courtyard and crashed into the wall. Others followed, clattering onto the flagstones all around them. The shaft of one spear struck Zana a glancing blow on the side of the head, forcing her to her knees.

"Go . . ." she croaked, swaying dizzily. "Go . . . while you . . . still can."

"Zana!" Nari cried, trying to get to her.

But Lal had her by the shoulder; his other hand closing around Rabon; all three of them vanished through the gate, out into the waiting darkness.

Chapter Sixteen
Forbidden City

The moon had set behind the nearest of the buildings. All they could see was a dull glimmer of moving water and high rooftops outlined against a scatter of stars. The rest was blackness, obscurity; the warm air, tangy with salt, closing about them like a moist blanket.

With Lal urging them on, they plunged forward, splashing through water that deepened with every step: its cool touch reaching up past their thighs, swirling around their waists and finally threatening to swallow them. Only Lal kept them afloat. Buoying them up, he strode on, pressing into the tide that frothed against his chest. While behind them, the noise and lights dimmed to nothing.

For a time the only sound was made by their own steady progress. Then, as Lal paused to get his bearings, they heard something else: the ominous plop of a heavy body striking the water; the swish and slap of a tail thrashing the surface.

Before Rabon or Nari could call out a warning, Lal veered off in the opposite direction. Half running, half swimming, he churned his way through the darkness, not stopping until he reached a stone ledge. Quickly he pushed Rabon and Nari onto it and dragged himself up beside them: the three of them huddled there, intent upon the water lapping the stone just beneath their feet.

When, after several minutes, nothing had appeared, Rabon sighed with relief and sank back against the stone wall.

"What do you think . . . ?" he began, and stopped as he noticed how tense and watchful Lal had remained.

He saw it then, the creature that had been there all along. Its dark color, its scaly back, blended into the water's rippled surface. Very slowly it was gliding toward them, its long snout inching nearer, its powerful body riding the sluggish current.

Rabon scrambled to his feet and started back. "Kill it!" he cried in alarm. "Kill it!"

But Lal, instead of springing into action, merely tipped back his head and made a humming sound, a high thin note which gradually rose and fell. A song — for that is what it was — that was foreign and at the same time oddly pleasing. Lilting and soft, a melody without any obvious beginning or end, it swelled out into the silence, somehow merging with the night itself.

The song's effect upon the creature was immediate. Mesmerized by the sheer magic of the sound, it opened its jaws and revealed its deadly rows of teeth in a strange act of submission. Its momentum continued to carry it forward, so that it nudged against the ledge, its gaping mouth only a hand's breadth from Lal's bare feet, but as if in a trance, it made no attempt to attack. Placid and still, it floated there like some creature made of wood, not moving until the cadence of the song changed slightly. Then in a flurry of froth and spray, it disappeared from view.

Wiping the sweat from his forehead, Rabon sank down onto the ledge. Beside him, Lal went on singing, not as loudly as before, but just as effectively. For although the night was no less dark, it now seemed less threatening. Rabon would have been glad had he not noticed how Nari had edged closer to Lal. She was sitting with her head against his side and seemed to have forgotten how ugly he was. Like the creature that had chased them, she appeared mesmerized by his soft voice — one arm thrown lightly across the great mound of his thigh, the other curled around his hairy wrist. And seeing them together like that, so content and still, Rabon felt suddenly excluded.

Alone. Cut off from the place of warmth and security that he had never quite known — or perhaps had rejected and lost.

"Can't you stop that noise now?" he asked harshly.

She turned slightly. "Hush! Let him sing," she said, and immediately resumed her former position, snuggled even closer against Lal's hulking body.

This time, to his surprise, Rabon felt a pang of envy, a pang so strong that he wanted to squeeze between them, to separate them forcibly. Instead, he drew away, farther along the ledge, and lay down alone, allowing the song to lull him to sleep.

When he awoke the sun had risen, and he wondered for a moment where he was. It was like the morning, weeks before, when he had woken in the swamp. Seen from within, in the early light of dawn, this too was a place of unexpected loveliness. Gone was the stretch of murky water; gone the hulking shapes of buildings brooding like monsters over the night. In place of that nightmare world, he was confronted by a place of light and color. The river rolling slowly past was almost as brilliantly blue as the sky. The buildings, even in the process of decay, had taken on a beauty of their own — the surface of the crumbling walls was tinged a mossy green; ferns and exotic flowers and tumbling vines sprouted from every crack and ledge. In among the vines he could just make out the diamond coils of water snakes, their glittering heads lifted to the sun. On the lower ledges a number of the crocodilelike creatures were basking in the growing warmth, their scaly bodies a deep greenish gold.

"Isn't it wonderful?" Nari called out to him.

As before, she was sitting close to Lal, her fresh young face alive with excitement. And again Rabon was touched by envy of this monstrous half-brother whom, until now, he had merely pitied.

"Yes," he answered halfheartedly, "it looks really . . ."

But Lal, motioning for silence, pointed over to their right, to where the Sun Gate was still in view. It had been lowered during the night, its vicious spikes pointing in toward them, preventing their reentry into Tereu.

"Must . . . leave . . . here . . ." he lisped warningly.

Rabon agreed. While they stayed close to the gate, they could easily be attacked. The problem was, which way should they go, because at that point the riverlike thoroughfare branched off in five separate directions. Even from where he sat, Rabon could see how some of those thoroughfares, in turn, soon branched or divided.

This, then, was the maze Zana had spoken of: a bewildering network of flooded streets that led the wanderer in endless circles. Rabon contemplated the beginnings of the maze gloomily, his eye falling by chance upon the building opposite the Sun Gate. Like all the buildings, its walls were covered with moss or festooned with vines. Yet down near the water's edge a small portion of one wall was clear of growth and covered instead by shiny tiles. They were a silvery color overall, but etched into them in gold was an intricate pattern of lines.

"What's that?" he asked Nari, pointing across the water to where the tiles shone in the morning light.

She shrugged. "Some of the priests say it's just a design. Others believe it's a map of the city. No one really knows."

"A map?" he took her up sharply. "Then why can't we use it?"

"Because it's unmarked. To use a map, you have to know whereabouts you are in it. Where to start. But the Sun Gate's not shown there. Nothing is. Even if it is a map, it's as confusing as the maze itself."

"But can't we work out where the Sun Gate should be?" he objected.

"People have tried," she explained, "but they can't agree because there are lots of places it *could* be. Like I say, if it is a map, only Luan can read it."

Only Luan. Was that really true, he asked himself? In which case, how had Jenna found her way through the city? Did she perhaps have Luan to guide her? Or . . . the word *guide* reminded him of the charm he wore around his neck. What had Jenna called it? "An ancient guide to those who are lost." And there had been something else that she had particularly wanted him to remember. It came back to him in broken snatches: ". . . the way . . . lies only where . . . where the sun cannot reach." Yes, that had been it: where the sun cannot reach. Yet how could that help him? What did it mean? And how did it relate to the charm he now wore? Or to the silver and gold pattern of tiles gleaming in the sunlight.

In the sunlight! What was it she had said? ". . . where the sun cannot reach." Cannot reach! Excited, yet still unsure, he peered more intently at the tiles. Although clear of growth, they were surrounded by a tumble of vines and flowers. Some of that lush growth, blown by the morning breeze, cast shadows across the maze of golden lines. Shadows! Dark shapes blocking out the sun!

With sudden insight, he grasped the secret. Understood what it was that Jenna, in her weakened state, had been trying to tell him.

"Lal!" he cried, and scrambled across to where he was sitting. "Your charm! Give it to me!"

No sooner had Lal drawn it over his head than Rabon snatched it impatiently and pushed the two halves together. There was a slight resistance, and then the clasps meshed with a faint click. Once again the charm was whole: a single design showing a two-headed snake joined by one sinuous body.

"The guide!" he broke out. "We have it!"

And forgetful of the water snakes and crocodiles, of the fact that he had never learned to swim, he leaped from the ledge.

The next moment he was floundering helplessly, the salt water filling his nose and mouth, stinging his eyes, sucking him under no matter how hard he tried to stay afloat. Coughing and spluttering, he was dragged to safety by Lal; the giant afterward carrying him and Nari across the flood on his shoulders.

In spite of his ducking, his sense of excitement remained—though he was careful, now that he was close to the gate, to keep his voice low. "Look!" he whispered, as he clambered onto the ledge close to the tiles. And holding the charm high in the air, he allowed the coiled shadow of the snake, cast by the sunlight, to fall directly onto the maze of golden lines. At first the two patterns seemed to have nothing in common; but then, as he revolved the charm, keeping its surface always toward the sun, the looping shadow locked onto a single golden thread that ran from one side of the tiles to the other.

"You see!" he said, pointing to the meandering line. "That's our

road. The one the sun doesn't reach. If we follow that, we'll get to . . .
get to . . ."

"To Luan?" Nari asked in a subdued tone.

He lowered his arm abruptly. In his enthusiasm, he had not considered where the charm might lead them. He had thought only of finding a way through the maze, of not being lost in the vastness of the city. But Nari was right. Where else would the path lead but to Luan? Hadn't Jenna said as much herself? "To the Night Lord or the Sun Lord, whichever one you seek." Those words, too, came back to him now. And for the first time they made sense—the looping path of the charm capable of being read backward as well as forward, from one snake-head to the other.

"Yes," he replied grimly. "The road that ends with Luan."

In his disappointment, he let the charm slip from his fingers. It struck the ledge and would have bounced into the water, but Lal shot out a hand and caught it.

"Luan!" he said in a husky whisper, and he held the charm up in its former position. Then again, with a thrill of discovery—"Luan!"— as he jabbed one huge finger at the point where the larger of the two snake-heads cast its shadow.

There was no hint of dread in his voice, his heavy features filled with a strange joy.

"What is it?" Nari asked, as amazed by his response as Rabon. "Do you want to go there? To him?"

"Home . . . for mother . . ." he lisped in delight. "Lal . . . take Jenna . . . home . . ."

"Jenna?" he queried.

"He's carrying her remains in that sack," Rabon explained. "He wants to bury them somewhere in this city."

He watched Nari carefully as he explained, expecting her to start away from the sack in disgust. Yet she appeared no more repelled by it than she was by Lal.

"And you think your mother belongs with Luan?" she asked Lal, placing a hand gently on his arm. "You're prepared to take her there? To face the Night Lord for her sake?"

He nodded vigorously. "Mother say . . . home . . . near Luan . . .

near water . . ." Again he turned toward the map, studying it, memorizing the shaded route they must follow. He nodded at last. "Lal . . . remember . . ." he said confidently, and reached out as if to lift Nari and Rabon onto his shoulders.

"Wait a minute," Rabon objected, fending him off. "Don't ask me to come with you. I'm here to settle a score with Solmak, that's all."

"How can you do that now?" Nari asked. "The Sun Gate's locked, from the other side. You couldn't even reach through, not with the spikes in the way."

"That still doesn't mean I have to give myself up to Luan!" he flared back, his voice rising, carrying across the water to the gate.

"Why not?" she pressed him. "You said yourself that Luan spared your mother. He may spare you too."

"What if he doesn't?" he replied—and again he was careless, letting his voice sound across the water.

He saw how she struggled with herself, having to gather all her courage before she linked arms with Lal—her golden skin in sharp contrast to his dark hairy flesh. "I'm prepared to take that chance," she said in trusting tones. "I'm sure Lal will protect us if he can. The way he did last night."

"If you're fool enough to believe he can . . ." he began, speaking as much out of jealousy as anger.

He was interrupted by raised voices on the far side of the gate. Someone shouted quite distinctly: "Fetch Solmak! Be quick about it!"

"Danger . . ." Lal murmured, a look of concern on his face. "Rabon . . . no stay . . . Lal say . . . come . . ."

This time he did not allow Rabon to object. Gathering both his young companions in his arms, he strode away from the gate, the blue water foaming in their wake as he breasted it.

Chapter Seventeen
Threading the Maze

The road they followed was narrow, lined by tall buildings, so that wading through the Forbidden City was like moving along green-fringed tunnels into which the sunlight filtered only dimly. In the deepest shade, clouds of tiny insects hovered above the blue water; crimson dragonflies flitted away at their approach; spangled lizards and water snakes, their jeweled eyes ever watchful, lurked in the tumbling foliage. And at every turn, basking in stray shafts of sunlight, there were crocodiles. Huge sinister creatures, they would flop into the water and glide forward, but always, as Lal's song sounded through the hot stillness, they would angle away, back to their sunlit ledges.

Nari, perched securely on one of Lal's shoulders, was entranced by everything around her. It was only Rabon who glanced fearfully at the crocodiles, as though doubtful of Lal's ability to keep them at bay. It was Rabon, too, who frequently voiced his anxiety about the route they were following.

"Are you sure it's this way?" he asked whenever they changed direction even slightly.

But once again his fears were ill-grounded, for at every fourth or fifth intersection they encountered another map of the city—the tiles always exposed to sunlight. And when they held the charm above it, invariably the shadow revealed that they were on course; following a single golden thread that coiled its way through the maze of streets.

After every such check, Lal patted Rabon reassuringly. "Lal . . . remember . . ." he insisted.

It was as well that he did, because later in the morning the wind began to rise, blowing a bank of cloud across the sun. With only Lal's memory to guide them now, they pressed on into the ever-freshening breeze.

By midday the water had grown choppy and the spray from small waves gusted into their faces; on every side the hanging veil of creepers was being blown into tangled shapes.

Drenched from head to foot, Rabon was the first to complain. "Can't we stop for a while?" he cried, rubbing his eyes that were stinging from the salt water.

Lal was about to turn aside and rest when he noticed something a little further ahead. Straight away, his forehead furrowed with concern, he began to sweep at the water with both arms in an effort to wade more quickly.

"What's the matter?" Nari asked him.

"Luan . . ." he croaked, making hastily for a sheltered alcove.

"Luan!" Rabon had ducked down instinctively, his eyes searching the alcove, half expecting some monstrous face to peer out through the shadowy cascade of vines.

But as Lal clambered, dripping, from the stream, all that confronted them was a series of reddish brown stains on the mossy stonework. Imprinted in the largest of these stains was the shape of a huge foot.

"What is it?" Nari asked.

"Blood, by the look of it," Rabon answered soberly, remembering how he had thrown the spear and heard it thud into living flesh somewhere beyond the gate. "Luan's blood, most likely," he added. "There's no one else here it could have come from."

Lal, having lifted his companions down from his shoulders, was crouched miserably among the bloodstains. He had begun to sing again, but mournfully now, groaning out a lament that was just audible above the roaring wind. The first few notes had barely sounded when there was a disturbance in the foliage and a water snake emerged.

Even before Rabon or Nari could yell out a warning, it had slithered up Lal's arm and settled one of its great coils about his neck. Not aggressively. Its touch as gentle and sure as Lal's own; its diamond-embossed head softly caressing his cheek as if to comfort him.

Nari, startled by the snake's appearance, had drawn closer to Rabon. He was glad of that: glad to have her there beside him, her hands clutching onto his arm instead of Lal's.

"Won't . . . won't it hurt him?" she ask uncertainly.

He shook his head. "I don't think so. He's used to them, and they seem to like him."

Already, to his regret, she had released his arm and moved a pace or two away, nearer to Lal.

"He almost seems to belong here, doesn't he?" she said in a wondering voice.

"That's because he was brought up in a swamp," he explained. "He understands places like this."

"So this is really home to him," she said thoughtfully.

"While Luan rules the Forbidden City," he reminded her, "it can't be home to anyone. Zana says it was abandoned longer ago than anyone can remember."

"Lal claims it was your mother's home," she countered. "In any case, Lal doesn't seem to be scared of Luan."

She had moved another step away, and he said quickly, "That's because he's stupid." It sounded harsh and unkind even to his own ears, and he added, "I mean he's . . . he's not . . . not very clever."

"Isn't he?" she said, challenging him. "Then why do we rely on him all the time? And why is he the only one who can remember the route we have to take?"

He had no answer to that and was left standing there awkwardly as she went and crouched beside Lal, not flinching when the snake also slithered about her neck, its heavy coils drawing her and Lal yet closer together.

Despite the steadily rising wind, they did not remain long in the alcove. Both Rabon and Lal were eager to leave, though for different reasons. And after drinking a little water from the skins, they moved off, following the same tortuous route as before.

For a while they made reasonable progress, with Lal slogging on, untroubled by the constant buffeting of wind and wave. But toward the middle of the afternoon they encountered a new hazard. The water level, which in most of the streets had reached only to Lal's waist, started to inch upward. Before long it was brimming around his chest, and then his neck, so that now the wind-driven waves were slopping into his mouth, the spray half blinding him.

Still the wind grew stronger. Shrieking along the watery gullies between the buildings, it tore whole colonies of vines from their ledges and sent them splashing down, where they immediately became yet another hazard: floating islands of living green that swirled along in the flood, threatening to carry Lal away.

It was in the midst of all this chaos that they saw the boat. They mistook it at first for one of the islands—a tangle of vines topped with colored flowers. Then, as it drew level with them, they were given a clearer view: it was a long, low craft laden with rows of woven baskets, each of the baskets filled with fruits and grains.

"The tribute!" Nari sang out.

Before it could be swept past, she leaped from Lal's shoulder and snatched at the rope trailing from the prow. She managed to grasp it, but was dragged under—her cry for help choked off; the boat stalling from her added weight.

With amazing speed, Lal sprang after her, his head and shoulders plunging beneath the surface. And all at once Rabon was floundering in deep water. He struck out frantically, and went under, a stream of bubbles spiraling up through the water above him. Desperately, he tried to follow them, clawing his way up, out into the thundering air. Near at hand, he glimpsed the side of the boat, and he clutched at it, missed, and went under again. Bubbles were pouring from his mouth now, whirling before his dazed eyes, exploding into nothing up there where this glassy green-blue world ended. For a split second, as he struggled after them, his mind felt as crystal clear as the bubbles themselves. He thought: Lal has deserted me. Somehow that seemed the most terrible part of all. Worse even than the panic and terror. "Bro—!" he started to shout. "Bro—!" The words pushed back down his throat; mouthfuls of water gushing after them, making him sink further. High above him, the last of the bubbles spun in upon themselves and vanished. Gone, he thought hopelessly, gone, and a cool green darkness closed in on him, dimming his eyes and mind together. Then, at the very edge of blackness, he saw it, up there in the wash of blue. A hand! Crablike and enormous. Thrusting down, fastening onto his hair, hauling him up and up, to where he was able to complete his earlier cry: "Brother! Brother!" The words, in between choking breaths, burst out of him as he lay sprawled across the side of the boat.

He was answered by a long wail of grief. A sound he had not heard since the night of Jenna's death. He jerked around, fearful that Nari had been drowned, but she was also lying in the boat, water streaming from her hair and clothes. The same wailing cry sounded again, more aggrieved than before. And this time he saw Lal's face as the giant floundered toward the boat's stern and began heaving on the rope: his features further distorted by grief, tears, and salt spray mingling in the drops that ran down his cheeks.

Rabon leaned toward Nari, attracting her attention. "Why is he so sad?" he half shouted.

She pointed to a red-brown stain on the side of the boat, where someone had rested, as if for support, allowing blood to drip onto the rough planking. ". . . Must . . . think . . . Luan . . . dead . . ." she yelled back, her voice just reaching him through the wind's roar.

"Dead . . . ?" he responded, shocked.

She nodded. ". . . Blood . . . boat adrift . . . what else . . . think?"

"Then he's crying for Luan?" he said, amazed, speaking more to himself than to Nari.

"What?" she called back.

But at that instant the boat slid out of the wind into the shelter of a porch and lodged against some steps. In that enclosed space Lal's wails were louder than ever, and Nari ran to the end of the boat and drew him down toward her.

"It's all right," she said soothingly. "The storm must have torn the boat from its moorings, that's all. Luan's probably just injured. He . . ."

"You sound as though you want him to be alive," Rabon broke in accusingly.

"And why shouldn't I?" she replied.

"Because we'll be safer with him dead. You know that as well as I do. He's the one real danger to us here."

"Lal doesn't seem to believe that."

"Well, I do! I hope Luan *is* dead. I . . ."

It was the only time Lal ever reacted angrily to him. Grabbing at the boat's prow, he shook it, sending Rabon tumbling over the side. Fortunately, the water was not deep there by the steps, and after a lot of splashing and struggling he managed to scramble out.

". . . not dead . . . ?" he heard Lal murmur hopefully. ". . . alive . . . ?"

"Why not?" Nari replied. "If he came this far, he can't be too badly wounded."

"Alive . . . !" he repeated eagerly. "Lal . . . find . . . help . . ." he added, already blundering into the water.

"But you can't go now," she protested. "It's late. It'll be dark soon."

He ignored her, pausing only to wipe the hair and water tenderly from Rabon's eyes. "Lal . . . sorry . . ." he whispered, brushing his rubbery lips against Rabon's cheek.

"Listen to me, Lal," Nari continued, pleading with him. "You won't be able to find anything in the dark. You'll only get lost. Why not rest here for the night? Eat something? You'll need to be strong to face Luan."

He hesitated then and eyed the baskets of food hungrily. "Lal . . . eat . . ." he agreed at last, and began cramming fruit and handfuls of grain into his mouth.

Thinking Lal had changed his mind about leaving, Nari and Rabon also started eating. After their long fast, the many different types of fruit and freshly gathered nuts tasted especially delicious. Yet they were given little time to enjoy their meal. Before it was half over, Lal again picked them up and prepared to depart.

"Come . . ." he lisped. "Find . . . Luan . . . now . . ."

Rabon tried to struggle free. "You're not taking me to Luan!" he shouted. "You can look for him yourself, without my help."

But it was like the moment when they had been within sight of the Sun Gate. "Rabon . . . no stay . . ." Lal muttered. "Danger . . . this place . . . Rabon safe . . . with Lal . . ."

And without further argument, he stepped out into the wind and spray.

In the short time they had spent in the sheltered porch, the water had risen further. After only a few steps, even Lal was out of his depth. To make progress, he had to keep to the sides of the streets. There, partly protected from the wind, clutching at vines and ledges, he half swam, half pulled himself along.

For Nari and Rabon, the worst part was crossing the intersections, when Lal was forced to strike out into the open water. Clinging grimly to his hair, half smothered by foam and spray, they were hauled along behind him. After each such crossing, Rabon begged Lal to stop, but with the light already failing, he only pressed on more urgently.

In the gathering dusk, the whole feeling of the city began to alter. Much earlier in the day, it had looked like a kind of paradise. With the onset of the storm, it had become more somber and gray, a place of discomfort, even of danger. Now, as the shadows lengthened, thickened, deepened into pools of black, it changed its character yet again: it grew slowly into that sinister world of nightmare they had been told of when they were young. No longer simply a city, it was transformed by the oncoming night into a realm of unknown peril, where fear and death, ever watchful, lurked in the gloom.

Soon, Rabon was clinging onto Lal's hair not just to stay afloat, but for comfort too. And when he glanced across at Nari, her young face pale and strained in the late twilight, he could see that she was no less scared. Only Lal seemed undaunted by his surroundings. His one concern was that they should not lose their way and at each of the intersections he dragged himself clear of the water and held on to some wind-blown vine as he peered keenly ahead.

Yet even Lal was startled by what happened soon afterward. Struggling into the very teeth of the storm, he had just rounded a sharp bend when all at once the night was filled with a regular booming noise. Like the beating of some monstrous heart, it was so loud that is sounded through the fury of the wind. A steady *thump, thump* that came not from any buildings, for there were none. In place of the network of streets, there was now only emptiness: a dark space of wind and water bounded by a looming smudge of utter blackness. It was from this blackness that the noise came: a pounding drumbeat that filled the air.

Lal had torn a section of stone from a nearby ledge and hoisted it above his head, ready to defend himself. Opening his mouth, he roared out a challenge. But no one answered. The regular *thump, thump* continued as before, oddly monotonous now that they had grown more used to it.

Nari was the first to realize what it was. "The sea wall!" she cried, pointing toward the line of blackness that cut out the stars. "We can hear the waves crashing against it."

Hardly had she spoken than a pinprick of yellow light blinked on high above them, somewhere near the top of the wall.

Lal, his faced raised to the wind, tossed the heavy piece of stone aside. He clutched at the sack hanging from his waist and held it up as if presenting it for unseen eyes to inspect. Then, sucking in his breath, he bellowed out a single word: "Luan!"

"No, Lal!" Rabon pleaded, trying too late to scramble clear. "Please!"

But Lal had already launched himself into the expanse of deep, storm-tossed water that lay between them and the towering wall.

Chapter Eighteen
The Moon Gate

To have released their hold on Lal's hair would have meant certain death for Rabon and Nari. Here in the open, the wind was too fierce, the water too deep, the smother of waves and foam too overwhelming for them to have survived for long. All they could do was cling in desperation, hoping that Lal's strength and determination would see them through. On every side they were surrounded by darkness and noise; watery hands wrenched at them; sharp talons of wind plucked greedily at their sodden clothes. And always, in the background, there was the shuddering drumbeat of the surf as it battered against the sea wall. The blown spray from that assault fell on them like heavy rain, the shriek of the storm like Luan's maddened scream—as though, in his insane fury, he had turned on his own dark domain in order to destroy it.

In all that confusion, there were only two things that remained stable: Lal's powerful body, ploughing tirelessly into the surge of wind and tide, and the speck of light, high above, toward which he was struggling.

After what seemed like an endless period of time, Rabon felt Lal's body steady beneath him. Then he was being dragged clear of the water and deposited on a broad ledge of streaming rock. The light was directly above them now, set high on the wall that was all that stood between them and the regular thud of the surf.

With Lal half dragging, half leading them, they made their way along the ledge and in through the lower entrance of a tall tower. Still they could see nothing; the empty spaces of the tower echoed to the storm's fury and to a cascade of falling water that pelted their up-turned faces. Working by touch alone, they groped through the blackness and located the beginnings of a spiral staircase.

"Luan!" Lal bellowed again, as if pleading with the gloom and emptiness that hung over them like some nameless threat.

But for the constant heart-pulse of the surf, there was no answer. And abruptly Lal lumbered upward; moving off so quickly, so eagerly, that Rabon and Nari were left behind.

"Wait!" they cried in panicky voices, scrambling after him, more afraid of being lost in that dungeonlike darkness than of what awaited them at the top of the wall.

Clutching onto Lal's tunic, they clambered up steps made for some-one much larger than themselves, winding slowly higher and higher to where the storm became a living thing, a mortal enemy, hurling itself furiously against the city. They knew when they were near the top by the feel of the stone beneath their feet: it was rocking and swaying, as if the whole tower were about to buckle and give way, to crumble into ruin.

Rabon could hear a voice, crying, begging: "No! No! No!" His own voice it was, so feeble and forlorn, useless against the demented screaming of the wind. A wind that suddenly buffeted him, caught him in its talons, and would have wrenched him away, flung him out into dark space, had Lal not drawn him close against his side where Nari was already held, secure.

They were up on the battlements of the wall, a sheer drop on their right, down to the city far below; the sea on their left—a series of giant waves, almost as high as the wall itself, marching toward them.

Blinking away the streaming spray, they found they could see the light again. It was on a level with them now, shining through a window space further along the battlements. Lal, his arms curved protectively about his two companions, was straining toward it. Head down, heavy

body slanted forward, he blundered at last against a closed door that
gave way before him. The three of them stumbled through the opening, into a dry windless place where the storm had not yet reached.

It took them a minute or two to recover. When Rabon next looked
up, he saw before him a long high-ceilinged chamber. In size, it was
more a spacious hall than a room. Lit by a single lamp, it was filled
with looming shadows. Among them, he was able to make out a row
of tall postlike objects lining the wall on the seaward side. One of
those posts, bigger than the rest, had a bulging, suggestive outline, as
if something were draped across it. That something—whatever it
was—seemed to twitch and move even as he gazed at it, and a
rumbling groan sounded through the chamber.

Rabon leaped for the door, only to be thrown back by the wind.
He glanced behind him, panicstricken, as the shape detached itself
from the post and stood upright. Its head was lost in the darkened
area near the ceiling; the stirring of its great limbs obscured the light,
throwing more shadows across the room. The edge of a shadow
brushed Rabon's face, like a dark stain on his pale skin, and he sprang
toward the door once again. But as before he was met by a wall of
wind that sent him tumbling back, rolling over and over until he jolted
against Lal's legs.

It was as he was scrambling up that he heard Lal murmur a single
word:

"Father . . ."

That stopped him. Steadied him. Made him turn and look as Lal
moved toward the towering shape that stood swaying before them as
though it, too, were caught in a strong blast of wind from the storm
exploding out there in the night. Repelled, and at the same time fascinated, his head half turned away, Rabon watched Lal take the shape
in his arms, lower it tenderly to the floor. As it settled, groaning, on
the hard stone, Rabon saw its face: as ugly as Lal's, but bigger, older,
gray with sickness. An outflung arm was caught in the light, and it too
appeared oddly familiar: thicker, hairier, more heavily veined and mus-
cled, but otherwise identical to Lal's.

"Help . . ." Lal called softly as he bent above the shape, his lips
quivering with distress.

But Rabon could not move, standing there transfixed, so that only Nari went to Lal's aid.

Between them, acting so gently that Rabon was filled with strange yearning, they eased the great shape over. A bloody patch in the middle of its back was revealed by the lamplight. There was another loud groan, this time from Lal. Unexpectedly it was echoed by a sobbing cry that broke from Rabon's lips. For there, lodged at the center of the bloodstain, was the shiny metal shoulder of the spearhead he had flung at Solmak.

Once, far away in his village (in another life, it seemed to him then), he would have been proud to declare himself the owner of that spear. Yet here, now, with the stone floor shuddering and Lal groaning in distress, he felt no triumph. To his dismay, he was beset by a sense of dread. As if, already, faced with the reality of the blood seeping from the living flesh, he had begun to guess at a truth he had not previously dreamed of.

Still fascinated, still repelled, he looked on as Nari tore aside the stained cloth of the tunic. The rest he lacked the nerve to watch. His eyes tight-closed, he heard Lal grunt as he tugged at the broken shaft; heard a gasp of pain swell out into the room. Then, after some frantic whispering, there was a rattle of hard objects striking stone . . . followed by silence.

Furtively, he opened his eyes. Jenna's bony remains now littered the floor, and Nari was pressing the empty sack to the gaping wound.

"It's all right," he heard her murmur. "The bleeding's almost stopped."

Lal had stood up. His face shadowed by the lamp, his eyes hidden in deep caves of darkness, he came over to Rabon and held something out to him. It was the spearhead, the point glistening with fresh blood.

"Take . . ." he lisped, his voice sad rather than accusing.

Rabon wanted to shake his head, to refuse it, but was not able to. His hand, almost of its own accord, was reaching out, accepting it as his own.

"I didn't mean . . ." he began, ". . . didn't mean to . . ."

He fell silent as his fingers closed around the shaft, the wood unexpectedly warm. Blood was trickling down from the point, splashing onto his knuckles. He tried to wipe it away, rubbing his hand and the spearhead on the front of his tunic, but the broad stain he left on the cloth only served to remind him of what he had done—the smudge of red like a mark of who he was.

"For . . . Rabon . . ." Lal added, and turned away.

Left to himself, Rabon crawled to a corner of the room and hunkered down, his face pressed bleakly to the wall.

He remained in that position for some hours. Behind him, Lal and Nari whispered together as they did their best to bind the wound. Later, a third voice joined theirs. At first little more than a sigh, it grew steadily louder, less hesitant, as if trying to match the mounting strength of the storm.

Listening to it, this voice so similar to Lal's, Rabon merely crouched lower, troubled more and more by feelings he did not understand. Feelings that stirred unwelcome memories. He recalled how Dorf, on the night of Lal's first appearance, had asked him in a shocked voice: "Do you feel nothing?" And then: "Damn it, she was your mother! . . . Even that thing out there knows what it is to mourn!" There were other memories too: of Jenna stroking his cheek with her gnarled hand, and of his violent response. Memories even of Solmak, of the father he had found and lost out there on the desert sand. Of the father he had come so far to kill.

How different it had been for Lal. Lal, who had made the journey burdened only by grief. Who had come all this way for another purpose altogether. And here at last, in this desolate place, he had succeeded in finding . . . had actually found . . .

Rabon shook his head, not wanting to finish that thought. Instead, he wondered bleakly: What have I done? What am I doing? There was no answer. Only a confusion of dread and guilt, and of loss too, that he could not cope with. It was almost preferable to turn again to the known reality of the spearhead, to allow the cool silence of the metal tip, pressed hard against his flaming cheek, to still the many voices jostling for his attention—including those soft and intimate murmurings that droned on behind him in the windswept chamber.

He had lost all track of time when Lal and Nari came to him. By then the storm was nearing its peak. The wind, it seemed, had grown into a merciless demon of vengeance, the waves into mountains of rock and steel that smashed everything in their path. Under their combined assault, the sea wall was creaking and groaning and threatening to give way as its stones ground restlessly against each other.

"That wall can't take much more of this," Nari was saying. "We have to help Lal if we're going to save it. And save ourselves, too."

"The wall?" Rabon looked about him with startled eyes, like someone waking from a dream. With a shock, he noticed how the lamp was swinging wildly, the violent pendulum motion keeping time with the slamming impact of the waves. "But the wall has always stood here," he objected. "It could never fall. Surely."

"It's still here only because of Luan," Nari explained. "He's the one who's kept the Moon Gate. Without him, the wall would have fallen long ago."

He looked at her in astonishment. Luan? The true protector of the people? Not the Sun Lord after all? No, he could not accept that.

"It's true," she insisted. "Everything we were told about him is lies. He's here to stop the sea breaking through and flooding the valley, to close the Moon Gate when the storms come. No one else could do it. They wouldn't have the strength."

"Then why . . . ?" he began.

"Why is it open now?" she took him up quickly. "He left it like that while he was away collecting the monthly tribute. He wanted to flush out the old city during low tide, to get rid of the stagnant water. That's part of his job too. Normally, he would have closed the gate again at the first sign of the storm, but he couldn't because of his injury. By the time he arrived back here, he'd lost too much blood. He was too weak."

Rabon, fully alert at last, had sprung to his feet. "So Tereu and the valley are being flooded?" he asked sharply.

"It's worse than that," she replied. "With the Moon Gate open, the wall is only half as strong as it should be. Unless we can close it soon, all of this" — and here she placed both hands on the trembling floor — "could be swept away."

Lal, who had been listening to their talk, reached out and touched

Rabon's shoulder. "Rabon . . . gatekeeper . . . like Lal," he lisped. "Rabon . . . help . . . now . . ."

It was the kind of appeal Rabon could not ignore. His eyes downcast, so he would have to look neither at Jenna's bones nor at the huge figure lying listlessly in the lamplight, he crossed to the line of four postlike objects at the far side of the room.

At close quarters, he could see they were not really posts at all, but metal levers, each emerging from a slotted hole in the floor.

Lal was pointing to the nearest lever. "Pull . . ." he instructed them. And the three of them together grasped the long metal handle and heaved backward.

For some seconds nothing happened, and even when the lever finally began to ease back, it did so with a slowness that left Rabon wondering whether he was just imagining the movement.

"Pull . . . !" Lal bellowed again, and they doubled their efforts, straining until their backs creaked and they were gasping for breath.

The lever was halfway along the slot now, poised between the open and closed positions. For a few moments, as they hung on to it, they felt as if they were lifting not just some mechanism beneath their feet, but the whole weight of the sea—each crashing wave sending dull vibrations up through their arms. "I can't . . . can't . . . !" Rabon grated out desperately. But at last the terrible weight was easing; the lever was moving again, gliding smoothly along the slot and clicking into place.

They knew they could not rest for long. Urged on by the ceaseless pounding of the waves, they were soon grappling with the second of the levers. Again, following their initial struggle, there were those few moments when they hung poised between success and failure, when they seemed to be pitting themselves directly against the unyielding power of the sea. Except this time the sea was almost too much for them: its weight made the lever jerk in their hands, like something alive trying to escape. Close to exhaustion, they very nearly let it go, gave it its freedom. Only Lal's last lunging effort swung the odds in their favor, and the lever reluctantly yielded and locked closed.

They were already half defeated when they grasped the third lever, so that even Lal's great strength was not enough to see them through.

Still too young for so heavy a task, he strained and struggled in vain. "It's no good!" Nari cried and was about to give up when a fourth shadow was cast upon the wall: a shadow more than a head taller than Lal's. An instant later, two mighty hands joined theirs; a grunt of pain mingled with their gasping cries as the sea grudgingly released its hold.

Almost too tired to care about the outcome, Rabon dragged himself over to the final lever. The monstrous shadow again loomed above him, but that, too, no longer worried him. Even when a dark hand brushed his arm, he barely responded. All he knew was that he must pull and pull and pull, until his own heartbeat and the thud of the surf merged into one. The sea surged through his veins, up into his brain, crashing against the cliffs of his skull. There it was, contained where it could hurt no one but himself, held captive in the sudden stillness of his mind.

It was that stillness that roused Rabon. Not silence, for the sound of wind and wave continued. No, there was noise enough. But at last the swaying of the room, the shuddering in the wall, had stopped. Relieved, he touched the floor on which he lay. To his surprise, it was pliant, soft; an echo of that dull wave-beat pulsing through it. There was a voice, too, rumbling up from somewhere beneath him, speaking words of endearment.

Puzzled, he raised his head . . . and looked straight into an ogre face. Bloodshot half-moon eyes, gaping black pits of nostrils, a swollen gash for a mouth—all less than an arm's length away.

He understood then where he was. Not lying on the floor at all. In his exhaustion, he had fallen across Luan's prostrate body. Before he could move, the giant lips whispered something he could not help but hear, words he had left far behind him, buried in the grave with Dorf.

"My . . . son . . ."

The words, the half-moon eyes, were directed not at him, but at Lal, who was crouching nearby. Yet that was no comfort to Rabon. With a stifled cry, he rolled clear and scrambled to the far end of the room.

Long afterward—for the rest of his life in fact—he wondered what it was that had disturbed him so. Simple fear of Luan? Jealousy of

Lal, perhaps, who had not been rejected? Or a hint of something else, of something more painful altogether?

Whatever the reason, he did not return to the lamplit area, but remained huddled in the shadowy corner for the rest of the night.

Chapter Nineteen
Invasion

He awoke, dazzled by bright sunlight pouring through the window opening. He could hear that the sea was still running high, the surf continuing to crash against the wall, but the wind had dropped to a strong breeze that cleared the atmosphere of salt and gave to the air a crystal quality.

His companions were still asleep, lying exhausted on the stone floor—as was Luan, his ogre face closed in pain and sickness. Yet as Rabon rose, those half-moon eyes flicked open; one of the treelike arms stretched toward him; the cracked lips lisped a single word:

"Water . . ."

He could not refuse, not with one of the leather waterbags still strapped to his waist, and reluctantly he upended it above the gaping mouth.

There was a grateful sigh. "My . . . thanks . . . Rabon . . ."

"You know my name?" he asked, surprised.

"Waiting . . . for you . . ." Luan murmured, speaking with the same slow difficulty as Lal.

"For me? Why me?"

Luan's immediate answer was to reach up toward him, as if to cup his face in one vast hand, but he shuddered back, out of reach.

"Yes . . ." Luan murmured with another sigh. "Not time . . . yet . . . not time."

Rabon wanted to ask him what he meant. Time for what? But Lal and Nari were stirring, disturbed by the voices.

At the sight of the waterbag in Rabon's hands, Lal nodded approvingly. "Rabon . . . good . . ." he said, chuckling with pleasure.

"Is he?" Nari asked, the mistrust in her voice making Rabon look away.

"Good . . ." Lal insisted. "Rabon . . . brother . . ." He moved forward and threw an arm affectionately about his shoulders. "Brother . . ." he repeated, and beamed down at Luan, as if expecting some word of agreement.

Instead, the Night Lord gazed pensively at them both, saying nothing.

Mistaking his silence for doubt, Lal stooped and gathered up the bones scattered on the floor. "Same . . . mother . . ." he cried. "Same . . . mother . . . same . . ."

He was cut short by a rumble of command from Luan. "Help me . . . must see . . . city . . ."

Luan was already struggling to his feet, his face so contorted by pain that Lal instantly forgot everything else. Laying the bones aside, he wrapped both arms around Luan's massive chest and helped him to the door.

The sight that greeted them, out there on the wall, was both beautiful and disturbing. The buildings of the Forbidden City, washed clean by wind and spray, were a sparkling green. Similarly, the network of flooded streets, flushed out by the surging tide, shone brilliant blue in the morning light. Those clear blue rivers, however, no longer lapped the lower floors of the buildings. They had risen alarmingly during the night, submerging some of the smaller structures altogether.

Like Lal and Nari, Rabon shaded his eyes and strained directly into the sunlight. What he saw, beyond the limits of the city, made him catch his breath: Tereu was also flooded. An arc of silvery water enclosed the whole town; stray arms of the same bright silver reached into the cultivated parts of the valley.

"We closed the Moon Gate just in time," he breathed out, relieved.

"If it had stayed open much longer, the whole valley would have gone under. The crops, the soil, would have been ruined."

"Yes," Nari answered, "though I don't expect Solmak sees it that way. He probably thinks the flood is a kind of revenge. The Night Lord's means of getting back at him."

She glanced at Luan as she spoke, but his eyes were closed and he was swaying wearily.

Seeing him like that, so weak and sick, Lal tried to lead him back inside, but he shook his head and began staggering toward the tower. He was too big, too awesome, to argue with, and between them they helped him down the long spiral stairs.

At the bottom, on the other side of the tower, was a doorway they had not noticed the night before. It led to a chamber even larger than the one they had just left. Here it was cooler, damper, and amazingly overgrown. Vines and creepers and multicolored orchids sprouted from the cracks in the walls. Much of the stone paving had been removed, and in its place grew a whole range of plants, from giant ferns to the tiniest, most tender of flowers. Lizards and water snakes peered from the thick foliage, their scaly bodies hidden, their eyes shining like precious stones in the greenish gloom. Only one of the water snakes was in full view: a gigantic creature, its body as thick as Lal's upper arm, it lay coiled on a moss-covered couch in the very midst of the tangled growth.

As Lal helped Luan onto this couch, the snake, its tongue flickering curiously, slithered onto its master's lap. Its cool touch caused him to rally slightly, and he placed one hand lovingly on the sleek head. Then his weariness possessed him once again, and he slipped away, back into exhausted sleep.

"Father . . . ?" Lal called hopefully, gently shaking his arm so that the snake raised its head and let out a hiss. "Father . . . ?"—his voice growing desperate when there was no response.

"Leave him," Nari said, drawing Lal away. "He needs rest, that's all. And food when he wakes."

"Food . . . !" Lal took up the idea eagerly, casting about for something to eat. When he found nothing, he lumbered over to the door. "Lal . . . get . . . food . . ." he declared loudly. "Bring . . . boat . . .

tribute . . . for Luan . . ." And before they could stop him, he ran outside and plunged into the water.

There was no point in Rabon or Nari trying to follow him. The water was far too deep for that. In any case, they knew that Lal was right: someone had to collect the boat and its baskets of food. In the meantime, all they could do was wait, sitting silently together in the gloomy chamber.

Rabon felt compelled to try to comfort his young companion, because she was clearly worried about Lal. But while he was still wondering what to say or do, she stood up restlessly and she, too, left the chamber.

He was tempted to follow her, uneasy about being left alone with Luan. That grotesque face, even in repose, unnerved him, made him think with longing of Dorf's homely features and loving smile. Yet for all that, he lingered there a while longer. Something Luan had said that morning — or rather, something he had almost said — intrigued Rabon. Approaching the mossy couch, he gazed wonderingly at the wart-covered flesh of the cheeks and nose; at the coarse hairline, so low on the forehead that it almost mingled with the eyebrows; at the tangle of hairs growing from the nostrils, the discolored teeth protruding from the mouth. For some minutes all he could see was the sheer ugliness of the features. Then, unexpectedly, he glimpsed something else: a suggestion of kindliness in the face too, despite its ogre appearance. A kindliness he would probably never find in the cold blue eyes of someone like Solmak.

Encouraged, he crept a little closer. "Luan," he murmured. "What did you mean, when you said it wasn't time yet? Time for what?" He took another step forward and stopped as the snake reared up in a warning show. "Is there something I need to find out?" he added in a whisper.

Slowly the eyes opened. The face, previously so still, like a sleeping mask, became alert, watchful.

"Rabon . . . not want . . . hear . . ." he lisped.

"Why shouldn't I? Is what you have to tell me so bad?"

"Not bad . . . only . . . truth . . ."

"The truth? About . . . about me?" he asked hesitantly, and moved back. For suddenly he was not nearly so sure that he wanted to hear any truths about himself from Luan's mouth. He could not say why that was so. He felt vaguely threatened by the idea, that was all. Unaccountably, even the kindliness in Luan's face had become a cause of unease, something to be escaped from.

As if aware of Rabon's dilemma, Luan nodded understandingly. "Truth . . . for . . . later . . ." he murmured, his eyes closing again as Rabon hurried from the chamber.

He found Nari sitting on the battlements. She was facing the city, staring into the sun, with the long lines of white-capped waves crashing into the wall behind her.

"Can you see Lal?" he asked.

"Yes," she answered shortly and pointed downward. Rabon barely had time to pick out the dark shape toiling along a flooded street when she raised her arm slightly. "But look over there," she said in a tense voice, her finger pointing now to the far side of the Forbidden City.

To begin with he could see very little, dazzled by the sun reflecting off the water. Gradually he grew accustomed to the glare, and all at once he stiffened and leaned forward. Something was moving out there. A boat, perhaps, making a V-shaped pattern in the water. Another such V-shape followed in its wake.

"Who is it?" he asked.

She shrugged. "Solmak and his guards, I suppose. Who else could it be?"

"But he's not allowed in the city. No one is."

"*We're* here," she reminded him quietly. "Why shouldn't Solmak come through the Sun Gate as well? He made the mistake of staying behind once before, when Jenna hid here. He's probably trying to wipe out that mistake now, and the flood has given him a perfect excuse."

"So he's after us?"

She shrugged again. "Possibly. Or maybe he thinks this is a good time to attack Luan, while he's wounded. Either way, he's a dangerous man. Wherever he goes, death soon follows."

Death! Rabon had learned from bitter personal experience how true that was.

"What will we do if Solmak finds his way here?" he asked nervously.

"Without the charm to guide him," she answered, "he doesn't have much chance of getting through the maze."

Rabon hoped she was right, but still he could not help worrying. Hadn't Solmak somehow found his way across the barren plain, discovered the one village he was seeking in all that empty space? So why should this city stop him? Given time, he might also discover the one golden thread that ran through the tangle of streets.

It was that fear, unreasonable or not, that kept Rabon up there in the blazing heat long after Nari had returned to the lower chamber. His eyes screwed up against the glare, he followed Solmak's steady advance, his spirits rising and falling at every twist and turn of the boats.

He left his lookout post only once during the course of the day—just before noon, when Lal returned with Luan's tribute. The giant was standing in the stern of the boat, his weight almost sending it under, his muscular arms propelling it along with a makeshift paddle. At his approach, Rabon ran down to help unload the baskets of food. He even stayed long enough to share a simple meal and to note, with oddly mixed feelings, how Luan was slowly recovering. Yet within the hour he was back up on the battlements, drawn there by his anxious need to plot Solmak's progress through the maze.

Late in the afternoon the boats passed behind a particularly tall cluster of buildings, and he lost track of them. Impatiently he scanned the surrounding streets, eager to detect some sign of movement while the light held. But already the shadows were lengthening, the twilight thickening into pools of darkness, and although he stayed there until the moon rose above the distant valley, the boats failed to reappear.

That was the most trying time of all: not knowing where they were; how close they might be. And throughout the early part of the evening, while Lal and Nari chatted together, he sat apart, sullen and unsettled.

Only Luan seemed to understand his plight, his eyes full of quiet sympathy. Once, he even motioned for him to come closer to the couch, but Rabon pretended not to notice—biding his time until the others settled to sleep, and then creeping back to the battlements.

The moon was half veiled by cloud when he emerged from the tower, so he saw the fire straight away: a clear beacon of flame shining out from one of the buildings. In so much darkness, it was impossible to tell how far away it was. Even so, to Rabon it appeared dangerously close. So close that his hand moved instinctively to the spearhead he still carried at his belt.

In a way it was that action that decided him: the cold touch of the metal reminded him that he had not left his village in order to hide or run away. His purpose had been to hunt down Solmak. In recent days—he saw the truth clearly now—he had lost sight of that purpose; he had allowed Solmak to turn the tables on him, to become the hunter instead of the prey. All that must change. There was nothing more to be gained by cowering at the limits of the maze. Like Jenna before him, he was only buying a little time, putting off the fateful day when Solmak would close in, when his boats would skim across the open water beneath the tower, much as his armed column had once marched upon the village. Neither city maze nor the barren plain were any real defense. Not in the end. The only way to survive against Solmak was to attack. To act like Solmak himself—someone without conscience or feeling. In that respect at least he would be his father's son. Much as Lal had proved to be Luan's son.

His mind made up, he lingered on the battlements until the first hint of dawn. As the stars began to fade, he took a last sighting of the fire, noting its exact position, and descended the stairs. The boat was waiting for him at the base of the tower, but he did not step into it immediately. There was one thing he had to do first.

On tiptoes he crept into the lower chamber. He remembered that Lal had been lying close to the far wall, Nari snuggled against him, their bodies overhung by sweet-scented vines. Gray light was seeping in from the doorway now, and he could just make out their shadowy outline. Silently, he stole through the foliage toward them and located the charm nestled in the thick pelt of hair that covered Lal's chest. No less carefully, he slipped it over the great dome of a head. Just before the charm pulled free, Lal half woke and reached up with one inquiring hand.

"It's all right," Rabon whispered. "It's only me."

There was a contented sigh. "Rabon . . . brother . . ." he muttered, and sank back into sleep.

With the charm hanging securely around his own neck, Rabon made for the doorway. When he was only halfway across the chamber, however, a coiled shape swung down and blocked his path; a flattish head darted toward him, making him draw back. Before he could recover, a giant fist closed around his arm and lifted him gently but firmly to the side of the couch. Even in the poor light, he could see the familiar half-moon eyes watching him, the lips struggling to force words past the swollen tongue.

"Stay . . . with us . . ." Luan murmured. "Safe here . . . Luan . . . Lal . . . protect."

"Let me go!" he replied in a tense whisper.

A hand brushed lightly against his cheek. "Rabon . . . not go . . ." The tone of the voice had changed, had taken on a pleading note. "If go . . . Rabon . . . die . . ."

"I don't care," he protested, struggling to break free.

The tone changed yet again, "Luan . . . care . . . always . . ."

Rabon had to fight down a desire to scream out a denial; to tell this creature from the darkness that he had no right to speak to him like this; to utter thoughts and feelings that rightfully belonged only to Solmak. To the father who had turned from him.

"Leave me alone!" he sobbed. "Please!"

Yet Luan, for all his care, was relentless. "Remember . . . Sun Gate," he lisped. "Rabon . . . try kill . . . remember . . ."

"You don't understand," he whispered desperately. "I threw the spear at Solmak. Only at him. I didn't mean to hurt you."

"Spear . . . wound . . . nothing . . ." Luan answered. "Rabon fight . . . Solmak again . . . that hurt . . . more . . ."

"No!" he objected, so loudly that Lal and Nari began to wake. "I don't want to feel hurt. I don't want any of that."

The voice was as insistent as ever. "What . . . Rabon . . . want . . . ?"

But he had no answer. What could he say? That he yearned for Solmak's loving heart? Or for his real bleeding heart pinioned on a spear? No. All he was sure of were the things he did *not* want: his last memories of Jenna, her gaunt body so wasted by fever she could hardly stand; Dorf's bones strewn across the desert sand; Solmak's eyes staring at him, empty of either pity or love.

With his free hand, he groped for the spear—knowing, even as he wrenched it from his belt, that he could not use it. Not here. "If you don't let me go," he blustered, "I'll . . . I'll . . ."

Thankfully, he felt the fingers slacken on his wrist. Something hard and smooth was pushed into his other hand.

"Take . . ." Luan was urging him. "If danger . . . blow . . . blow . . ."

Then he was free, running for the door and out into the bleak gray dawn.

Chapter Twenty
Hunters and Prey

Early morning mist hung heavy in the air as Rabon paddled across the open stretch of water toward the first of the streets. The object Luan had given him—a large seashell with a blowhole bored in one end—he had tossed carelessly into the bottom of the boat. At that moment he was far more interested in the charm that hung around his neck, for he reasoned that it was his true lifeline: his one chance of finding Solmak and emerging from the maze alive.

Not that he was yet able to use it. For that, he needed the sun. So at the first intersection he tied up and waited.

The sunrise was not long in coming. The first yellow rays were soon arrowing between the buildings, dissolving the mist that hovered cloudlike above the still water. As the last misty shreds swirled and vanished, he stood up and searched eagerly about him. Yet the hoped-for silver tiles, with their crisscross of golden threads, were nowhere to be seen.

Disappointed, he made a mental note of his exact position and moved on. He was similarly disappointed at the next intersection, and the next. Nowhere in this part of the city, or so it seemed, were there any maps.

It was only after repeated failure that the truth occurred to him.

The recent flood had done more than submerge the lower buildings: it had also covered the maps. If any existed hereabouts, they lay far beneath him, down in the greeny-blue depths.

For the first time since setting out, he hesitated. The question now was whether to play safe and turn back, or to push on and give himself to the maze much as Solmak had done. The thought of being lost and alone somewhere in this city, especially at night, caused him to shiver. Even so, he needed only a minute to make up his mind. Flinging the charm into the bottom of the boat, where it lay beside the shell, he plunged the paddle deep into the water and drove forward.

From then on he navigated by guesswork. Lacking Lal's formidable memory, he made no attempt to remember the path he was taking. He concentrated instead on keeping to an easterly course. And then, when he estimated that he had come far enough, he struck off toward the south, heading for the spot where, by his own reckoning, Solmak and his men had spent the night.

Whether by luck or good judgment, he at last succeeded in reaching a cluster of buildings similar to those he had sighted from the wall — though down at water level it was difficult to be sure that this was in fact the area he was seeking, especially as there was no sign of Solmak. The watery streets branching out all around him lay undisturbed, and the green-swathed buildings gave no hint of what they might have witnessed only minutes earlier. From the surroundings alone it was impossible to tell whether anyone had . . .

He stopped halfway through that thought, suddenly suspicious. Still there was no positive evidence of Solmak's having passed this way, yet Rabon's keen young eyes had noted a strange kind of absence. Until the previous ten minutes or so, he had spotted numerous crocodiles sunning themselves on jutting windowsills and ledges. Some of the bigger ones had even followed his boat for a while, attracted by the scent of prey. Now the streets were empty, with not a crocodile to be seen, as if they had all been enticed away, lured by a human scent so strong that . . .

He dug in his paddle and brought the boat swinging round. So Solmak had traveled along here! But in which direction? Again the street itself offered no clue. He had only his instinct to go by, and his instinct told him that if Solmak were hunting the Night Lord, he would favor the west. Wasn't that where the sun sank from view? Where the night began its reign?

He turned the boat and, with the sun shining hot on his back, he resumed paddling — more urgently now that he had some hope of success. A hope that was soon rewarded, for within the hour he spotted what he was looking for: a long reptilian back showing just above the surface of the water a short way ahead. More of those knobbly backs appeared as he speeded up: a whole flotilla of them, all moving along the street in the same direction. And now he could detect something else. Voices! Low and persistent to begin with, murmuring among themselves. Then one in particular, louder and more strident, stood out from the rest . . .

He had already veered in toward the side of the street, where the cascading vines gave him ample cover. It was as well that he did, because at the next bend he saw them: two boats floating side by side in the middle of an intersection.

Pulling his own boat in beneath a thick drapery of growth, he tied it up and peered out. As far as he could tell, there was some kind of argument taking place on board the other craft. The soldiers were grumbling or glaring sullenly; Pendar was waving his arms about and shouting. Only Solmak appeared uninvolved. Sitting quietly in the stern of the nearer boat, he was staring straight before him.

In that position, with his back turned toward Rabon, he would have offered a perfect target had he been closer, but the distance was a little too great. To be accurate over that range, Rabon needed to be higher.

He glanced up through the tangled vines and noted that the unflooded part of this particular building stood only a few stories above the water level. Moreover, there was a gaping window space within easy reach of where he now stood.

He made this decision instantly, and seconds later he was scrambling through the window into the dusky green interior. Somewhere in the gloom, a heavy-bodied lizard lumbered off, and in his eagerness to give it a wide berth, he stumbled upon the staircase he was looking for. It was rickety and half crumbled away, but it held his weight and he quickly mounted toward the rectangle of blue sky.

When he emerged into the sunlight, he found that although part of the roof had fallen in, the outer parapet was still intact. This too was overgrown, offering him ideal cover, and he crept around it until he was again overlooking the street.

The boats were in clear view now, but Solmak was no longer sitting down with his back turned invitingly. He had moved to the middle of the boat, in among his men; he had also entered the argument.

"You have nothing to fear, I tell you!" he was shouting. "Luan is a man like any other. Didn't the boy wound him?"

"I still say we turn back," a soldier answered from the other boat.

Solmak rounded on him angrily—and the sudden movement prompted the viper coiled around his arm to rear up and hiss. "Are you scared of a mere man?" he asked in a scornful voice.

"It's not just Luan I'm scared of," the soldier retorted. "It's this place. Like an endless road leading nowhere. If we don't get out soon, we'll die here."

"Die?" Solmak repeated mockingly. "I see no danger."

The soldier had leaped to his feet, making the boat rock alarmingly. "How can you say that?" he shouted, pointing to the crocodiles encircling the boats. "Just look around you!"

Solmak surveyed the waiting reptiles, a thoughtful expression creeping over his face. When he again turned to the soldier, all trace of anger had vanished.

"So you're refusing to go on," he said coldly.

"I am."

"In that case, the time has come for us to part company."

"Part company? I don't see how—"

But Solmak had already nodded at Pendar, and before the man could finish, the priest grabbed one of the paddles and struck him hard across the side of the head.

The soldier went over the side without a sound, his body-armor dragging him under. While the crocodiles were still closing in, he managed somehow to struggle to the surface and clutch onto the boat's gunnel.

"Help me!" he shrieked.

Again Solmak nodded, and Pendar, as dutiful as ever, stamped on the man's hands. He fell back and the crocodiles had him — their green-gold bodies writhing together as they tore at his living flesh, a red cloud billowing out through the blue water.

Rabon, looking on, had forgotten about staying under cover. Too shocked to think clearly — his face deathly pale, his mouth dust-dry — he had risen to his feet and was standing in full view of those below. He was noticed straight away and some of the soldiers pointed and cried out even as their companion perished.

Those cries — so familiar and ordinary compared with the horror he had just witnessed — were what roused Rabon from his numbed state. Below him, Solmak was groping for one of the spears stowed in the bottom of the boat. Rabon had to act fast: there was no time to retreat along the parapet, and now, more than ever, he understood what he could expect if he stood there passively. That left only one alternative, and snatching the spearhead from his belt, he flung it hard.

It was an ill-timed, hurried throw — he realized that almost before the spearhead left his hand. Helplessly, and with a new sense of horror, he watched as it flew over Solmak's shoulder, straight toward the other boat. While it was still a blur of silver in the air, soldiers began leaping aside, tumbling over each other in a desperate attempt to avoid being hit. And miraculously they escaped; the weapon passed harmlessly between them and buried itself in the wooden planking.

Only then did the real danger present itself. In their haste, the soldiers had upset the balance of the boat, which was heaving and swaying. They tried to steady it, but only made matters worse. One gunnel dipped beneath the surface, allowing water to gush in. Frantically, they scrambled to the other side, plunging it deeper still. Water was swirling around their knees now, the craft pitching out of control.

"Keep still!" Pendar was roaring.

But the weight of the water alone was enough to make the boat tilt crazily. It rolled once . . . twice . . . and finally, with an almost lazy motion, turned over completely, spilling the soldiers into the jaws of the waiting crocodiles.

Rabon did not see the first part of the carnage. Just as the boat was turning over, he was distracted by the flash of Solmak's spear passing beneath his outflung arm. It left behind a sharp, burning sensation, as though someone had laid a white-hot iron rod across his ribs. With a grunt of surprise, he clamped a hand over the wound, the pain making him stagger and lose his footing. From the corner of one eye, he glimpsed Solmak's face, turned not to his dying men, but raised triumphantly toward Rabon. Then, with a sick feeling of despair, he was falling, his body twisting, catlike, in an effort to save itself; his mind telling him over and over that to enter the water meant death—a death far more terrible than any Solmak could deal out.

That terrifying certainty helped to save him. It gave him the strength to cling onto the vines that were scratching his face and arms, tearing at his clutching hands. His palms burned and scored, he tightened his grip and slowed his body to a halt.

Glancing down, he saw a crocodile nosing toward him and quickly he jackknifed upward, out of reach. There was a windowsill not far from where he hung. He reached it by half swinging, half climbing through the vines and drew himself into the opening with a sigh of relief.

It was a relief that was short-lived, for when he turned back toward the street, the scene below was far more horrible than anything he could have imagined. A mass of gleaming reptile bodies churned the water; faces, hands, gaping wounds showed above the surface for an instant and were gone; the once blue depths had become a bloody tide spreading rapidly outward. And worse still, the catastrophe threatened to include the second boat.

A few of the soldiers, Pendar among them, had fought their way through the carnage and were pleading to be taken on board. Pendar himself was beaten back by Solmak, who was interested only in his own safety. But some of his men tried to save the other victims. Their efforts made the boat heel dangerously, and the crocodiles did the rest—the great jaws snapping at outstretched arms; the heavy bodies lunging clear of the water and landing athwart the boat itself, causing it to crack and split.

Solmak was the last to leave the foundering craft. He was standing on the prow when it slowly upended. Gathering his strength, he launched himself outward in a graceful dive that carried him deep beneath the surface — his armor-clad body knifing down through the thrashing limbs and disappearing, as if rushing to meet a death he could no longer avoid.

The whole hopeless struggle was over within minutes. Though not for Rabon. Cold and trembling, despite the growing heat of the day, he was still standing at the window when he heard an ominous dragging sound on the stairs. He guessed what it was without needing to look: one of the crocodiles, as yet unsatisfied, coming in search of fresh prey.

"No . . ." he whispered. "No more."

He was not rejecting death alone. What he found harder to endure was the idea that the horror should continue. With a shudder of repulsion, he climbed out of the window and down toward his boat, which still lay hidden among the vines.

Had he remained in the building a few seconds longer, or glanced back even once, he would have discovered that the noise on the stairs had not been made by any crocodile. The face that appeared at the head of the stairwell was human enough: blue eyes clouded slightly by recent contact with salt water, golden hair slicked back and dripping wet. Stripped of his armor, his upper body adorned only with a coiled viper, the man padded across to the window and looked out.

From his vantage point, he noted the bloody wound in Rabon's side; the way the boy gasped with pain when he gripped the paddle; how, after only a few feeble strokes, he half collapsed into the bottom of the boat.

"Yes," he murmured approvingly.

But Rabon had struggled up, and now there was something else in his hands. A curved, shiny object that he raised to his lips, his cheeks puffing out as he blew. There followed a deep booming sound that rang out loud and clear, that carried through the still, hot atmosphere and reached to the outermost limits of the city.

The man, looking on, did not wait for a reply. He was already clambering from the window and lowering himself carefully onto an upturned boat that had drifted in against the side of the building.

Chapter Twenty-One
"Love Those You Fear"

R abon must have blacked out. He realized that the moment he opened his eyes. For one thing the sun was much higher, almost directly overhead, and beating fiercely down upon his back and neck. Also, the air was filled with a noise like distant thunder: a low rumbling that was strangely out of keeping with the brilliant sunlight.

Groaning from the pain in his side, he clambered to his knees and looked around. To his amazement, he saw that the boat was moving, drifting quite rapidly past lines of buildings. There was nothing propelling it but the water itself, which was flowing like a river. At the next intersection several such rivers swirled together before surging away in a westerly direction, and the boat, bobbing and rocking in the current, was carried with them.

The rumbling noise was louder now, closer, the current moving a little more swiftly. And Rabon, trying to gauge his speed and direction, noticed something else: the general water level was lower, as though this moving river were draining the worst of the flood from the city.

Draining the city? That puzzled him for a few seconds, and then the truth dawned on him. This was the answer to his cry for help, to the note of distress given out by the shell. Not thunder at all, but the constant crash of water. Someone had opened the Moon Gate and, with the sea levels much lower now that the storm had passed, the floodwaters were escaping. All he had to do was stay in the boat and he would automatically be carried through the maze and back to his companions.

Relieved, he lay down on the hot planking and allowed himself to be borne along; content, for the time being, just to listen to the way the rumbling grew ever louder.

Not until it was almost deafening did he look up again. The boat had emerged from the maze of streets and the wall was directly ahead; the salt-whitened stones loomed up at an alarming rate as the boat was sucked seaward.

With difficulty, for the wound jagged painfully whenever he moved, he rose to his feet. What he saw before him made him cry out in fear. For in the shadow of the wall, where tiny waves had once lapped gently, there was a hill of broken water, and at its base, a foam-streaked whirlpool.

He barely had time to cling on before the boat plunged downward. The very speed of its descent drove the prow under, and immediately the whirlpool had it in its grip, dragging it around and over. Rabon, thrown violently sideways, caught a fearful glimpse of the gate itself: its great steel prongs like gleaming tusks in the darkness of the water. He reached up, clawing at the air in a last attempt to survive . . . and discovered a face hovering above him. A face no longer ugly and deformed — not as he saw it then. The bulging eyes, the warty flesh, the protruding tongue, had somehow acquired a beauty of their own. All he wanted to do, in that split second before the water closed over him, was go on gazing at them, forgetful of how they had once made him shudder with disgust.

"Lal!" he wailed — that name, all he had time for, expressed the many things he had never said or even thought until that moment.

Then, as the boat was drawn under and the water rose almost to his chin, he was grasped by the hair and tugged upward.

He was not conscious of the tearing pain in his scalp — only of being freed from the whirlpool's dragging grip, of being clasped against a firm strong body.

"Lal!" he sobbed again.

The answer was lisped so softly that he had to strain to hear it above the roar from the gate: "Safe . . . Rabon . . . safe . . ."

His eyes pricking with tears that still he could not shed, he was carried past the tower and down into the lower chamber. There, Lal placed him carefully on Luan's lap, handling him as gently as if he were a precious gift.

Again, he did not flinch away. For Luan's face, like Lal's, appeared far less hideous. After what he had witnessed that morning—so much senseless cruelty—these heavy features no longer repulsed him. The sadness in the half-moon eyes, although puzzling, was also a welcome sight: proof that the real nightmare lay not in this gloomy chamber, but out there in the sunlight.

"Who . . . did . . . this . . . ?" Luan asked, pointing to the bloody gash on his side.

"Solmak," Rabon confessed. "He tried to kill me."

The great head was thrown back, the flared nostrils quivering with emotion. "Where . . . Solmak . . . ?" he demanded, his voice strangely muffled.

"He's dead," Rabon answered, and his voice, too, seemed to catch in the back of his throat as if he were speaking words for which he was yet unprepared. "He and his men were killed," he went on. "The boats overturned and the crocodiles . . . they . . ."

"Dead . . . !" The huge body beneath him, holding him, had begun to tremble; the face suddenly became an agonized mask of sorrow. "Brother Sun . . . dead . . . !"

"Do you mean Solmak's your brother?" The surprised question came from Nari who had also entered the chamber and was standing beside Lal.

Luan did not reply immediately; his face turned away while the trembling in his body slowly subsided. "Brother Sun . . . gone . . ." he murmured bleakly, and wiped the tears from his cheeks. "Now . . . only Luan . . . only . . ." He fell silent, too upset to continue.

What roused him was the constant dull rumble from the Moon Gate. With his head cocked, listening, he swung warily toward the source of the sound as though seeking out some familiar, long-term enemy. "Gate . . ." he murmured, and nodded at Lal. "Must . . . close . . . must . . ."

"He's still tired from opening it," Nari objected before Lal could respond. "It was so heavy. He needs to rest before going up there again."

She was not exaggerating. Lal, normally so ready and eager, was standing there listlessly, his heavy shoulders drooping with exhaustion.

But still Luan shook his head. "Must . . . close . . ." he insisted, and tried to rise, only his weakness forcing him back. "Water . . . protect . . . city . . ." he explained. "Protect . . . from Tereu . . ."

"From Tereu?" Nari asked sharply.

"Yes . . ."

And straight away Rabon knew that this—the reverse of all he had ever been taught—was the truth. The terror did not originate in the moon-washed darkness of the Forbidden City. Nor was the Sun Gate built to contain Luan, whatever the people of the valley might say. Like the flooded streets, it was there to keep the people themselves at bay.

"Please, Lal," he said, adding his voice to Luan's, "you have to close the Moon Gate. You *have* to! If the streets dry out, more soldiers will come. And then . . ."

There was no need to say any more. Lal had already placed one hand gently on Nari's mouth, silencing her. "Lal . . . go . . ." he replied, and limped toward the door.

Confined to the chamber by his wound, Rabon did not see how Lal struggled with the terrible weight of the gate; how, with Nari to help him, he wrestled with each of the levers in turn—his chest heaving, his muscles stretched to the utmost, his face torn by strain and exhaustion. Those wrenching labors registered themselves down below only as a series of grinding noises, and then as an abrupt silence, when finally, the fourth section of the gate locked into place.

By then Lal was lying senseless on the stone floor, so that he, like Rabon, failed to witness one other important event.

It had begun minutes earlier, when an upturned boat, with a man clinging to its underside, had emerged from the city and come racing across the open water. Just before it reached the whirlpool, the gate had closed, so instead of being sucked under and destroyed, the boat had merely bumped against the base of the wall, and the man, unharmed, had climbed onto the lower walkway.

The first Rabon knew of his presence was when the doorway suddenly darkened. He looked up, expecting to see Lal or Nari, but the man standing there was older than either of them, and sickeningly familiar. Even in the poor light, and stripped of his body armor, there was no mistaking his identity. His long blond hair and the viper coiled around his upper arm left no room for doubt.

"Solmak!" Rabon breathed out—and rolling clear of Luan, he staggered to the center of the chamber.

Instantly it was as if his long journey from the village had never occurred. He might almost have been back there on the barren plain, standing outside the village gate, facing Solmak as he had once before. Because nothing had really changed: the same blue eyes regarded him coldly; the full-lipped mouth was twisted into the same mocking smile.

"So we meet again," Solmak said easily. "After our last little encounter, I thought you'd be less eager to greet me."

"I'm not here to greet you," Rabon answered, trying to sound threatening despite his aching wound and empty hands. "I'm here to finish what I began. To make you pay for the things you've done."

Behind him, there was a murmur or protest, followed by a soft moan as Luan struggled to his feet.

"The things I've done?" Solmak asked in the same mocking tone.

"To those men out there!" Rabon half shouted. "And to Dorf! To him especially!"

"Dorf? What kind of name is that?"

"The name of the man who brought me up!" Rabon cried angrily. "The man I now call my father. Yes, father! Not you! You're not my father anymore!"

There was a shuffling step behind him and another soft moan as Luan almost slumped to his knees, then recovered.

"Me? Your father?" Solmak responded, and gave a bitter laugh. "Is that what Jenna told you?"

"Yes . . . that is . . . she . . ." He faltered, unsure of what she *had* told him. So much of what had passed between them during their last conversation had been so vague, even misleading. Hadn't she insisted that his father would never fail him? Rabon had only to gaze into Solmak's eyes to realize how untrue that was. And there had been the warning she had sounded: how he must fear those he loved and love those he feared. Fear those he loved . . . Yes, that made more sense: it suggested that Jenna had guessed how Solmak would act. Yet if she had already guessed, why had she also . . . ?

"Well?" Solmak prompted him, breaking in upon his confused thoughts. "Did she say I was your father or not?"

"In a way . . ." he began uncertainly. "I mean . . . she didn't exactly mention your name. Nobody did." The plain truth of his last words seemed to slam into him, rocking him back on his heels, as though he had been physically pushed. "But everyone in the village knew it was you," he added hastily, a note of desperation in his voice. "Everyone. They didn't need to say your name."

"So it was just rumor," Solmak said with a knowing smirk.

"But I look like you," Rabon rushed on. "The same hair, the same eyes, the same . . ."

Again he faltered, Jenna's words echoing in his mind: "Fear those you would love . . ." Except that now they alerted him to the gold-hilted dagger protruding from Solmak's belt. Instinctively, he began inching away.

"Why shouldn't we look alike?" Solmak asked slyly. "After all, we're closely related."

"Take . . . care . . . brother . . ."

The warning came from Luan who had shuffled another step forward, one giant hand stretched out toward Rabon.

"Care!" Solmak snarled. And all at once the dagger was in his hand, causing Rabon to stumble backward. "Of a brat that isn't mine? A brat that would take the power of the Sun Gate from me?"

"Not yours . . . ?" Rabon was no longer retreating; he was standing exactly between the two men, as if held there by invisible forces.

"Haven't you realized the truth yet?" Solmak jeered.

"Enough . . . !" Luan bellowed.

But Solmak shrugged aside the objection, the knife flashing dangerously. "Jenna rejected me," he went on, all the old bitterness and jealousy welling up through his voice. "She preferred that thing there. She chose *him* as her husband!"

"But you said—"

"I've told you!" Solmak shouted, his blue eyes suddenly flecked with red. "She rejected me! Me! I'm only your uncle!"

"Then . . . then . . ."

Momentarily, Rabon forgot about the danger. Forgot about everything but this one revelation. Cold with shock, all he could do was stand there, helpless. And it was then that Solmak struck: the dagger plunged downward as he leaped to the attack.

Rabon glimpsed the point descending and at the same instant he felt himself being wrenched clear and sent rolling across the stone floor.

He rose unsteadily, blood oozing afresh from the wound in his side. Through a veil of pain, he was aware of some kind of struggle going on in the shadowy depths of the chamber. A giant form swaying drunkenly; a smaller, paler figure thrusting upward. A glittering point of light spun away and landed with a clatter on the flagstones.

He shook his head, and as his vision cleared, he realized that what he was watching was not really a struggle at all—not now that Solmak had been disarmed. Luan was down on one knee, making no effort to defend himself; while Solmak, his face contorted with fury, was punching at him with both clenched fists.

"Brother . . ." Luan was murmuring. "Brother . . ."

For a moment it seemed as if Solmak were responding, for he drew back, but only in order to slip the viper from his arm and hurl it straight at Luan's throat.

It struck with unbelievable speed. Before Luan could brush it aside, it had sunk its fangs three times into the soft skin of his neck.

"Sweet dreams, dear brother," Solmak sang out, and broke into laughter. "You'll be rejoining your beloved Jenna sooner than you'd think. She's already waiting—"

He broke off as Rabon leaped forward, flailing with his bare fists much as Solmak had done moments earlier. And with the same result. Weakened from loss of blood, his blows had little effect. There was a dull explosion somewhere inside his head, and once again he was sent rolling across the stone floor.

This time he found it almost too painful to move, and for a while he lay there gathering his strength and courage.

On the far side of the chamber, Luan, already in the grip of the poison, had also fallen. He was slumped against the sea wall, his arms hanging weakly at his sides, his half-moon eyes narrowed to mere slits.

"Rabon . . ." he called, so softly that his voice hardly carried across the chamber.

With an effort, Rabon struggled to his feet. The faint cry sounded again, and hesitantly, drawn by feelings he could not ignore, he took one step, and another . . . and felt his foot brush against something hard. He looked down and saw the dagger lying at his feet—flung there during the initial struggle. Solmak had spotted it, too, but before he could retrieve it, Rabon had stopped and gathered it up.

The gleam of the steel blade, the feel of the gold-embossed hilt, seemed to stir something inside him: a long-held anger that flared anew, forcing him to shift his attention away from Luan, back to the hated figure of the Sun Lord.

"You!" he rasped, and began to advance, the dagger held out before him.

For the first time since he had entered the chamber, there was a look of fear in Solmak's eyes. "Think before you act," he said in a husky voice. "There are two gates. Not one. We don't have to fight over them. The Moon Gate I give to you. It's yours. This monster here can't last much longer."

Monster! The word struck Rabon like a blow. And he slashed with the knife, the blade narrowly missing Solmak's neck as he started backward.

"The Sun Gate then!" Solmak gasped.

He slashed again, the point piercing Solmak's cheek and slicing across it.

"Both of them!" Solmak cried, one hand held to his cheek. "I'll give them both to you! My word on it!"

But it was not that promise that made Rabon pause. It was the stir of movement in the foliage beside Solmak's head; the sinuous movement of a body thicker than the tree from which it hung.

"The gate of death," Rabon whispered as the deadly, jeweled head slid into view. "The gate . . ."

"No . . . !"

The faint protest came not from Solmak, but from Luan. In spite of the effects of the poison, he had managed to stand upright.

"No . . . !" he cried again, his voice so weak it was like the sighing of the wind. And he pointed first to the knife and then to the jeweled head hovering in the foliage.

"You mean spare him?" Rabon said incredulously. "Let him live?"

"Live . . ."

"But after what he's . . . he's done to . . ." He took a gasping breath, unable to express the words that trembled on his tongue. "And Dorf too . . ." he added desperately. "The way he killed . . . killed both my . . . both my . . ."

Still he could not say it aloud, could not bear to confess what he could no longer deny. Somehow it was easier to strengthen his grip on the hilt of the dagger; to turn, ready to slash yet again; to drive Solmak beyond the final gate, where even Luan's mercy could not reach him.

Yet he had delayed too long. There was a strangled cry, and as he swung around, the dagger poised in his hand, he saw the first slithering coil, like a gilded rope, tighten around Solmak's throat. A second coil slid around his chest, and then a third. The whole jeweled body was convulsing now; each spasm produced a cracking of bone and sinew. Solmak's eyes, no longer blue, were bulging horribly, threatening to burst from their sockets. His once handsome face, in those brief moments before death, had grown more deformed than Luan's.

"Help . . . him . . . !" Luan pleaded.

Help him? How could he? Hadn't he, Rabon, made the long journey from his village for just this purpose, to witness Solmak's death throes?

Luan's shadow lurched across his line of vision.

"Must . . . save . . . brother . . ."

Yes, Rabon thought secretly, brothers. The two of them. Like Lal and me. Solmak's face, too, no longer handsome: the tongue ballooning from the mouth; the nostrils flaring unnaturally; the goggle-eyes straining outward — the sheer hideousness of the features appealing to him, as if this were Lal himself begging for mercy.

He would have acted then, but Luan had already intervened. With his remaining strength, he tore the snake away and clasped the lifeless Sun Lord to his chest. "Brother . . . !" he sobbed — for the last time, with his last breath. The two men crumpled to the floor; their bodies — one golden smooth, the other dusky dark — twined together in death.

Rabon had not moved. He was staring at the two bodies, the tears in his eyes making them swim together, merge one into the other, until he could no longer separate them. He blinked, and as the first scalding drops ran down his cheeks, he fell forward and threw his arms around Luan's lifeless form.

"Love those you would fear," Jenna had warned him, but he had not listened, had not understood. And now . . . now . . .

It was like a gate opening inside him: the grief flooding through, as relentless as the sea at the height of the storm. There was no holding it back. And for the first time in his young life, he wept uncontrollably. Not just for Luan, but for Dorf and Jenna — and for himself too.

He was still lying there crying when Lal reentered the chamber and scooped him up in his arms. He did not struggle or pull away. As Lal also raised his voice in grief, he clung to the giant body with all his might; holding on for dear life, as though he feared that Lal, too, might slip away into the darkness.

Chapter Twenty-Two
The Gate Between

While Rabon rested, allowing his wound to heal, Lal and Nari busied themselves with the task of collecting wood. There was plenty of it to be had—heavy branches and half-rotten logs that had been carried in by the storm and left lodged in the window spaces and doors of buildings when the waters receded. Using Solmak's boat, which Lal had righted, they ferried the timber through the streets and back to the wall where they carried loads up to the battlements. It was there, in full view of the city and the sea, that they built the great funeral pyre.

To begin with, Nari argued that they should place only Luan and Jenna's remains on the pyre. Solmak's body she wanted to hurl into the sea. There had been a time when Rabon would have agreed with her; but now he hesitated, remembering how Luan had died with the word *brother* on his lips. Finally, at Lal's insistence, they included Solmak—the two dead brothers and the woman they had both loved lying together on the heaped wood.

They did not light the fire until the evening of the second day following Luan's death. The moon was close to full by then, and they waited until the upturned faces of the dead were brushed with its soft silver light before thrusting the brand into the pyre. It burned slowly for the first hour, but as the heat dried out the timber, the fire grew brighter, and soon sparks and jagged flames were shooting high into the air — so high that they seemed to reach almost to the moon itself.

For more than half the night the fire burned. The three companions grouped sadly around it, watching as the faces and limbs of the dead glowed with a final, borrowed heat, and slowly faded. In the early hours of the morning the fire also faded, sinking to a dull red glow that blinked out just before dawn.

There was no need to dispose of the ashes. As the sun rose above the distant mountains, a brisk wind blew in from the sea. Gathering force, it lifted the fine ash and sent it drifting out across the city, the tiny particles swirling and twining together in the brilliant light of early morning.

"Home . . ." Lal declared. "Home . . . for Jenna . . . for Luan . . ." Although he sounded sad, there was an undertone of acceptance in his voice.

Rabon also felt compelled to say something, especially about Dorf and Solmak, both men important to him in such different ways. But somehow, still, he found it hard to bring the two extremes of his feelings together.

"Maybe . . . maybe there are only two great gates after all," he said at last, as the wind continued to lift the ashes and whip them out into the sunlight. "Gates that everyone has to pass through, whoever they are and whatever they're like. Gates that no one can keep."

"Solmak tried to keep them," Nari reminded him. "Don't forget that. He thought he could decide who should be born and who should die."

"That was his big mistake," he conceded.

Nari's eyes were fixed keenly on his face. "Do you think you'll ever make that mistake?" she asked quietly.

He moved closer to Lal, taking comfort from the giant's presence. "Not if Lal stays with me," he said. "He'll help me remember that the Sun Gate's just a gate. Nothing else. Between the two of us, we can even get rid of it, bring the two cities together again."

It was with that intention, less than an hour later, that they set out:

Rabon and Nari sitting in the boat and Lal wading on ahead, the rope from the prow draped over his shoulder.

Jenna's charm had been lost days earlier when their own boat had been sucked through the Moon Gate, but that did not seem to worry Lal. Having found his way through the maze once, he now had it firmly committed to memory. At every intersection, he knew immediately which direction to take. And as he strode on, his high piercing voice rang out through the streets, mesmerizing not only the crocodiles and snakes, but also Rabon and Nari, who sat dozing in the growing heat of the day.

He woke them late in the afternoon, when the Sun Gate first came into view. It was raised, with armor-clad guards positioned in the opening and on the wall above. Some of the guards began brandishing their spears when they sighted Lal, and for a second or two Rabon half believed it was a sign of welcome. Yet there was nothing welcoming about the shouts that drifted across the water. They spoke only of hatred and fear—words like *monster* and *devil* being used again and again.

Sensing what might happen next, Rabon urged Lal to hurry, but before they could reach the gate, it closed with a crash, and most of the guards ran off. Those that remained lingered only long enough to hurl their spears wildly at Lal, and then they, too, disappeared.

The rows of vicious spikes made it impossible for Rabon or Lal to raise the gate from their side. All they could do was sit in the boat and wait, calling out occasionally in the hope that someone might hear. But nobody came until close to sunset. As the long shadows of buildings reached across the water toward them, there was a bustle of activity in the courtyard beyond the wall, and slowly the gate rattled upward.

In the glare of the setting sun, they saw Zana and a small group of old or aging priests standing in the opening.

"So," Zana said, smiling happily at them, "you all survived. Did Luan protect you?"

At the mention of Luan, Lal drew in a sobbing breath, and it was Rabon who had to reply.

"Yes, he protected us from the storm, And from Solmak, too."

"Solmak!" Zana dropped her voice to a whisper, her eyes darting warily from side to side. "He left here some days ago, with two boat-loads of soldiers."

"It's all right," Rabon assured her. "He won't be coming back. He's dead."

"Dead?"

"They all are. Luan, Solmak and the men he took with him. They were killed . . ."

He stopped as several of the priests sank to their knees. Even Zana had lowered her eyes and bowed her head.

"Then you are the new Sun Lord," she said in a respectful tone.

"No," he responded decisively. "There'll be no more Sun Lords. From now on this gate remains open. People can go into the Forbidden City if they want. Eventually we can drain the streets, make the houses fit to live in."

"What about Lal?" she asked quietly. "Where will he live?"

"Here with me," he said passionately — recalling in that instant how Luan had appealed to Solmak with his dying breath. "We're brothers. Twins. We belong together. There shouldn't be any walls or gates between us."

Zana gazed thoughtfully at him before slowly shaking her head. "I fear you're asking too much," she said. "You saw how the guards reacted. The people will never let Lal stay. To them, he'll always be a monster. A creature of nightmare. As far as they're concerned, he belongs out there, in the darkness they dare not enter."

Rabon's cheeks had begun to flame angrily. "I still say Lal stays," he insisted, reaching up and taking Lal's hand in his. "If I have to, I'll *make* the people change their minds."

"What?" Zana asked sarcastically. "Do you mean order them? How can you, if you're not a Sun Lord?"

He saw the trap into which he had fallen. "I'll persuade them then," he added lamely.

"What will you say?" The question came from Nari, the doubt in her voice undisguised.

"I'll tell them what he's really like. How he looked after me and saved my life. Once I've explained that to them, they'll start to see him differently."

"How long did it take *you* to see him differently?" she asked in the same doubting voice.

He winced, exactly as if she had thrust her hand against his wound. "But that was different," he protested. And to prove his point, he ran over to the stairs.

Above him, in the deep shadow of the wall, there was a stir of movement. Indistinct figures gazed down to where he stood, drenched in the dying rays of the sun.

"Listen!" he shouted. "I've brought the new Night Lord to live here in Tereu. He won't hurt anyone. He's—"

He got no further: a few warning spears sailed down the stairwell and drove him back.

Yet still he refused to give up. Grabbing hold of Lal, he urged him forward. "See for yourself!" he cried. "He's a friend. He's my—"

This time the spears were flung in earnest, one of them grazing Lal's neck and leaving behind a thin red line.

"What are you trying to do?" Nari screamed. "Have him killed? Is that what you want?"

She had dragged Lal to safety—she and Rabon, each holding on to one of his hands, tugging in opposite directions.

"You have to give them time," Rabon was arguing.

"Time for what?" she was shouting back. "To plot his death?"

It was Lal who brought the argument to an end. Shaking free of them both, he stepped back. "Lal . . . go . . ." he bellowed.

There was sudden silence, the sun at that moment dipping out of sight, plunging the courtyard into near darkness.

"Go?" Rabon asked in a small, hurt voice.

Lal nodded regretfully. "Leave . . . this place . . ."

"Do you really have to? Couldn't . . . couldn't you . . . ?"

The giant bent down and pressed his forehead against Rabon's. "Brother . . . must . . . go . . ." he lisped in his tenderest tones. "Keep . . . Moon Gate . . ."

"But you'll be so alone," Rabon murmured unhappily. "There'll be no one to . . ."

"I'll be with him," Nari cut in.

She spoke with such conviction, with such unmistakable devotion to Lal, that to Rabon it was like hearing his own voice. And he wanted to declare loudly that he too would leave Tereu, accompanying them back into the Forbidden City, spend the rest of his life in willing exile. Yet, noticing how they gazed fondly at each other, he said nothing. They had no real need for him any longer, he could see that clearly. Were he to go with them, *he* would end up as the lonely one.

"I could stop you," he said foolishly, struggling with a bitter sense of disappointment. "Keep you here with me."

"You mean act like Solmak?" Nari asked.

That comparison hurt, because he was still certain of one thing at least: come what may, he would never do anything to harm Lal.

"All I meant . . ." he began miserably. "All I was trying to say . . ."

Lal, with his usual understanding, reached down and brushed the newly formed tears from Rabon's cheeks. "Tereu . . . not home . . . for Lal . . ." he explained simply. "Home . . . for Rabon . . ."

It was not a rejection, only a statement of fact that Rabon could not deny. For, with Dorf and his old life in the village gone forever and with his place at Lal's side now taken by Nari, Tereu *was* the only home left to him.

"Go then," he said in a dejected voice. "Go if you have to."

Yet, having dismissed them, he could not bear to witness their departure. That would have been asking too much. His eyes streaming tears, he turned from Lal's outstretched arms and faced the darkness of his own city. Deaf to Lal's cries of farewell, undeterred by the spears that clattered onto the flagstones all about him, he strode toward the stairwell.

There was nothing brave about his action. Had one of the spears pierced him, he would have welcomed it. Not that he was consciously seeking death. Overcome by emotion, he hardly registered what was happening. In a kind of daze, he looked on blankly as Zana rushed forward and shielded him with her own body while she made his identity known. He remained equally unresponsive when the guards, dropping their weapons, hoisted him onto their shoulders and bore him triumphantly through the streets. Some time later he was dimly aware of people calling out and cheering, of smoky light falling onto a sea of happy faces. But what it all meant, he had no idea.

When he finally came to himself, he was standing alone on the steps of a tall building. The city was quiet again, the streets dark and deserted. In place of his blood-stained tunic, he now wore a long yellow robe, and there was a chain around his neck with a golden key hanging from it. His right arm also felt peculiar, heavier than usual, and when he glanced down he saw that a viper was coiled about it.

"What . . . ?" he cried in alarm—and tearing the snake loose, he threw it onto the steps.

A familiar figure immediately emerged from the nearby shadows. "There's nothing to fear, Sun Lord," Zana reassured him, and she picked up the snake and held it out. "The creature is only half grown. Harmless. Its venom and its love for you will develop together."

He pushed the animal away. "I don't want its love," he said resentfully.

"What *do* you want?" she asked in a humble voice—speaking not as a friend, but as a servant whose duty it was to obey.

He looked around him, as though searching for an answer to her question. Not far from where he stood, he could see the wall, its spiky top silhouetted against the moonlit sky.

"The Sun Gate . . ." he muttered. "That's what I want. Take me there."

"But Lal and Nari have gone," she reminded him gently. "Hours ago. They left at sunset."

Her words, instead of dissuading him as she had intended, served only to reawaken his sense of longing.

"Take me there just the same," he insisted.

Obediently, she led him through the silent streets that once they had both fled along, and down the stone staircase to the courtyard.

The gate had been lowered and locked, and his first impulse was to use the key—to disappear through the opening to leave Tereu and all its responsibilities far behind. But while he was still fingering the golden chain, Zana said firmly:

"They have each other, Sun Lord, like Luan and Jenna before

them. They need no one else. All we can do is leave them in peace. That much we owe them."

He knew she was right, although it hurt him unbearably to admit it. And releasing the key, he gripped the bars of the gate with both hands.

Before him lay the Forbidden City. Not dark or threatening, but drenched in moonlight. The air was still, the water mirror smooth, and in its depths there floated a perfect image of the moon. Full and round, it stared back at him like an all-seeing eye, like part of a face he had known and learned to love, and finally lost. While he stood there gazing at it, a faint breeze ruffled the surface of the water, causing dark streaks of shadow to ripple and flow. One of those shadows, much larger than the rest, seemed to grow into a living being that moved toward him, its hand raised in greeting. And suddenly he was straining forward, pushing so hard against the gate that the metal links drove painfully into his cheeks. But already the breeze had died, and as the water settled, so the shadows retreated, leaving the night as empty as before.

Beside him, Zana reached out and touched his arm, as though trying to still the shiver of disappointment that ran through him.

"There's a saying amongst the people of the sun," she muttered. "When someone longs for the impossible, we say they're wishing for the moon."

Was that truly what he longed for, he wondered, the impossible? Or was it something far more real? Something he had held, had at last come to cherish, and then had torn from his grasp.

Unable to prevent himself, he began to cry, the tears running down his cheeks and splashing onto his yellow robe. With the tears came a series of remembered images: Lal rescuing him in the swamp; Lal carrying him across the desert and later standing alone in the gully while the great boulders rumbled down; Lal's giant shadow half filling the cave when he had saved him from Boran's axe; Lal protecting him from the intense cold of the mountain passes . . . And so they went on, one image after another flashing across his mind. But most of all he recalled Lal himself. His face. A face he now yearned just to look at once again.

Pressing his own face against the bars at the gate, he gazed up at the placid beauty of the moon.

"Farewell, Brother Night," he whispered forlornly. "Farewell . . ."